Ferro family

THE ARRANGEMENT 23

The Ferro Family

By

H.M. Ward

LAREE BAILEY PRESS
www.HMWard.com

amazon

COPYRIGHT

LAREE BAILEY PRESS
First Edition: MARCH 2017
ISBN: 9781630352219, 9781630351335, 9781630351533 (Paperbacks)
ISBN: 9781630351328, 9781630352202 (eBooks)

THE ARRANGEMENT 23

CHAPTER 1

The gunshots echo in my mind as I stare out the window, down at the pool. Crimson streamers seep from the two bodies lying face down in the water. I recognize Sean's form, the sweep of his shoulders and his thick dark hair. The hardened stiffness of his stance, the remorse and grief he bore, is now absent as he floats, listless.

There's nothing surrounding me at that moment. There are no towering walls lined with bookcases. The scent of expensive rugs and feather filled furniture alludes me. The voices around me get sucked into the void that holds me firmly at its center. Vic cackles behind me, but it sounds like static in my ears. My body flushes hot before turning to ice.

All this time, I wanted to be like Sean. I wanted to feel nothing, to have the ability to be a cold, sadistic bastard if required. I wanted to patch myself up and shut the world out, but as I tried to learn those things from Sean—I fell in love with him. It wasn't supposed to happen. I knew I couldn't bear to have my heart ripped out again. Now that the moment has come it doesn't play out the way I'd imagined. I don't fall to the floor in a hopeless heap, unable to control my tears. No, instead fury races through me, but it's tempered by something that slithers through my mind—a single thought woven from the last cobwebs of my shattered soul. The delicate nature of it instantly turns to steel.

The effect is like slamming a door. Staring at Sean's lifeless body does something to me, and I change. The spider-web-thin cracks that have covered me for so long fracture. The freefall begins and I know I'm about to tumble beneath the surface of my mind, to whatever darkness lies beneath.

Emotion drains from my body as if poured out hastily. The fear vaporizes and is swept away like a cloud of smoke. There's nothing left after that point. The voice in my head, the one that tells me to hope and press on no matter what is silent. She's not screaming at me to run, to fight, or do anything. There's a void in her absence, an empty black chasm filled with icy darkness. Is this the nightmare I've had so many times? I dreamed of getting pulled under and drowning. The water was a noose around my neck, unrelenting, unforgiving. There was no way out, but when Sean was there, the dreams faded. Tonight it feels like that dream is a reality. No one can save me. I may still be among the living, but I've already perished. I'm below the surface and breathing water, and the strangest thought occurs—I'm not afraid.

Shifting my gaze from Sean's body below, I glance out of the corner of my eye at the man responsible for my misery. Vic caused all my pain and suffering. He's too close, grinning at me with that bloated snake of a mouth. His shaved head has a halo from the chandelier above, making him appear as a demented, dark angel. He's rubbing his palms together slowly, waiting for me to fall apart before his eyes.

Miss Black, who has been unconcerned so far, unsteeples her fingers and lifts a brow. Lips slightly parted, she leans forward from behind the desk. It's the equivalent of dancing on a desktop for someone like Black. The woman never moves, never reveals what she's thinking, but she recognizes the change in me. It takes a woman that devolved into a monster to notice the breaking point. Black remains silent. Her attention cuts to Vic as she sits back again to watch how I play out my hand.

I'm not a mastermind. My wrath is nothing compared to Sean's. My vengeance is a basket full of puppies compared to Mel's. And Henry—who the hell knows why he's so fucked up, but I can't blame him anymore. Even for that night when he nearly killed me. It's impossible to know what's going on behind their eyes when a person breaks.

That moment is now. I sense it. Shard by shard, my tattered soul obliterates until nothing remains. The calming silence, the empty echo within, is deafening. There's no sensation of heat or cold against my flesh, no recognition of the silk fabric caressing my skin. That piece of me broke a moment ago. Cognitively I recognize the fact, but I still can't process it.

Instead, I stare at my brother and realize he doesn't know what just happened. He doesn't sense the newly formed soulless creature in front of him. He expects me to cry, to lash out in hatred, and fall to the floor in a crumpled mess of sobs. He's practically giddy as he waits, but the moment never comes.

Marty clears his throat and tucks his chin at the same time he clicks his heels together. I can think with calculated calmness, which should be frightening. The person who can make calculated moves after having her heart ripped out is not a life worth saving. I make no attempt to clutch the crushed pieces of my spirit. Holding onto the shards will only cut more. I'm done with this. I feel the thoughts snap into place like a plastic puzzle. The path I want to take is clearing, but I need a few moments to put it all together and make sure it works.

I buy time by turning to Marty and glare into his brown eyes. "You fooled me twice, you sonuvabitch. It won't happen again."

Vic practically squeals with delight and presses his callused fingers to his mouth to contain his excitement. My brother's mannerisms unnerved me before tonight. That high pitched squeal would send my hair standing on end. Now it does nothing.

Vic throws his arms to his sides and steps towards us, placing a hand gingerly on my arm as if we are old friends. I don't shake him off. He catches my eye. "An idea, if you will, little sis. A challenge of sorts. What if I gave you the chance to pay him back for his lies? For his deceit?"

There's no way out of this room other than to walk out with them, so that's what I need to do. It should pain me, and I should feel torn, but I don't. Betrayal doesn't strangle me, and there's no tremor in my fingertips, not anymore.

I hold Marty's gaze while I answer my brother, "How?"

Vic grins as he glances between us. He retracts his palm from me before he folds his arms across his chest before pacing a slow circle around us. He lifts his fingers and rubs his chin before purring, "An eye for an eye. It's only fair, and that's what life is all about, isn't it, Masterson? Fairness. Nothing else matters because nothing else resonates as deeply as being unjustly mistreated." He stops behind me and takes a step forward.

I should want to run, to panic, but I don't. No emotion is present, and it seems like it doesn't matter what Vic does, I won't feel anything.

Is this how Sean felt all day, every day? It's like there's a protective layer surrounding me, boxing me in. This is what I wanted from the moment my parents died. A protective box, a wall around me that no one can penetrate. The only problem is that it's suffocating me. But it's not like a lack of air in my lungs. Rather, it's as if I boxed myself into a coffin and I pulled the lid shut. I should be terrified of that thought, but it doesn't make my heart race or my skin sweat. The wall around me is what separates the people from the monsters. This is why Sean gave in, why he did what he did with the call girls— why only certain things made him feel again.

All this time, I thought Sean could be redeemed, but I can see things from this side of hell. There's no way out. No wonder he fought so fiercely to keep me from becoming like him. All this time, he knew there was no life after breaking like this.

Vic's hands land softly on my shoulders, his pinky moving in circles on my bare skin. He purrs next to my ear, "And seriously, Avery—how many times can the same man lie to you without consequences?"

I don't shake him off. I don't feel sickened by his touch even though I know I should. Instead, it's just there, another dead sensation. Miss Black continues watching in silence as Vic stands behind me.

I stare at Marty while he holds my gaze, expressionless. "It's been too many times."

Marty flinches slightly at my icy undertones. It seems like his eyes are trying to speak, but they fall on deaf ears. A storm is building inside of me. Pieces of incomplete thoughts swirl like dust rising from the ground, obscuring the full picture. I let the segmented thoughts twirl and float.

All this time, Marty has played both sides. That's the object in the center of my mental dust storm. Marty killed Sean. He wasn't the one to fire the gun, but his betrayal is the reason Sean's dead. Marty's loyalty has never been to me. I see that now. Every calculated move he made was to lure me closer and drop my guard. I leaned on him, cried in his arms, and slept in his bed. Every step of the way was a path paved with lies.

Vic steps back and strides behind Marty. He rolls the black bead between his thumb and forefinger before pocketing the bracelets. Tipping his head to the side, he sneers at Marty. "Are you ready to prove where your loyalty lies once and for all?"

CHAPTER 2

Marty's voice is clear and unwavering. "My loyalty has always been with you."

"Sometimes I'm not so sure and this little task will prove your allegiance once and for all." Vic glances at the men behind Marty. "Give me that crazy woman's knives. Do you know how many she had on her?" He says it to me as if I knew where Mel stashed blades on her person.

I don't but play along, allowing my mind to turn my plan over again and again. Poking holes in it, and patching it back together. I mutter, "She probably has more."

Vic shakes his head as he folds his arms across his chest tightly. "Not a chance. We checked every inch of that whore's body."

A tall, wide man nods and retreats out the door at the far end of the massive room. His footfalls disappear, but I count them before they vanish. Mel is close by, but I can't hear her. She's either dead, or they're holding her somewhere.

Vic flips a grin my way. "Well, not me personally, but my men are thorough. Maybe we should pat you down, little sis." He arches a brow at me.

I stare at him with no expression and lift my arms at the same time I spread my legs. "Go ahead."

The sparkle in Vic's eyes burns out. He frowns and swats a hand at me. "You're no fun when you're like this. I expected you to be bawling your eyes out on the floor." He stares at the rug and pouts. "You have no idea how much I've wanted to slam my foot into your ribs and feel them crack." When Vic glances up, he adds with a smirk, "I guess that I'll have to save that for later."

The threat rolls off me. I wonder if I'll feel pain. Right now, I'm pretty sure I could rest my hand on a stove and not feel my flesh burning. While that sense appears to have perished, I notice other things, minutia. They're the kind of things that usually don't matter. No one examines every grain of sand on a beach, but for some reason, that's how I see things now.

Black is still pristine, sitting fully erect, and her fingers curled as her hands are clasped calmly in front of her—except her ring finger. The nail touches the desk, ticking off the seconds, scraping into the wood. I don't look directly at her, but I can see her out of the corner of my eye. There's hardly a sound from that movement. Her red nails disguise a trickle of blood from her nailbed and across her pale fingertip. She pushes on that sharp splinter again, making no other movement, no indication that she cares about anything. There's another bead of blood. I thought she was neurotic before today, but now—I'm not so sure. Pain increases focus and she'd need it if she's swimming in a sea of apathy. There are monsters at the bottom of the ocean. Now that I'm down here, they aren't scary.

How far gone is Miss Black? That's the question. I can recognize my own kind, and there's no doubt about Vic—but Black is still a question mark.

A thought sears through my mind, flashing brightly. Sean. He did what he did— he manipulated dread and power to feel. He'd been so disconnected from his body that he used sex and terror to channel his emotions, to cause a burst of light in the darkness. It's not as terrifying to have done those things with him now. Back then it was, but I was afraid.

What happens when there is no fear? If fear is dead, what am I capable of? If nothing burns inside my chest—not vengeance, compassion, or kindness—what compels me to act? I don't know. But from the swirling thoughts in my mind, the only thing that I'm certain of is that I want to get to Sean's body and take him far away from here. I want to hold him one last time and say everything I never said—I want to tell him about the baby. It doesn't matter that he's already gone, that he'll never really know. My thoughts latch onto an image of me holding his lifeless body in my lap, telling him about our daughter and planning a future that we'll never have.

Three lives were stolen today. There's no way to save her, to keep the baby within me safe. That thought rings clearly, with utter certainty. Even if I could escape, I'm not running from this anymore. There will not be a third generation of Stanz women who spend their lives running and hiding. I've already accepted that. If I could feel, I'd keep fighting for her—I'd hope my way into delusions that would never come to pass. There's no way to protect this child from the monsters in this room, which only leaves us with one exit.

Vic cackles as he tells me the rules and places his sweaty palm on the center of my back, pressing his flesh against my bare skin in a way that's not brotherly. Leaning in close he growls, "This is your chance to show me what you're made of, little sis. If there's any trace of the family blood running through your veins, it better pop up now. You never know, it could change my mind. I could make different plans for you." His eyes slither over my body as he says the last sentence.

I remain stiff and don't reply. With a shove, Vic pushes me into the corridor. Black rises and trails behind, walking next to Marty, eyeing him as if she hasn't sized him up properly. We walk down the carpeted hallway with Vic's men in tow. As we pass quietly by paintings and priceless art, I catch sight of a white animal at the end of the passage—it has huge white furry haunches, massive paws, and a very round rump. From a distance, I recognize the beast. Vic really has a bear, and it's roaming the hallways of his house. No one comments on the animal or acts like they're worried about it. The beast is walking away from us, which is fine by me. Who the hell owns a pet bear?

Golden light flickers from antique looking gas lamps lining the walls every few feet. The flame is housed behind glass and perched on a bronze fixture within. The chandeliers in the alcoves are electric and throw off more light. Then, we're back to gas lamps with red walls that illuminate the space in warm hues that seem to dance as we pass. I wonder if those fixtures run through the entire house.

Before I have time to consider it, Vic shoves us through a pair of glass doors that lead to the back lawn. "Loyalty is something that is defined by actions, not words." Sprawling green goes all the way back to the shadows at the edge of the property where the tall trees jut up into the inky night sky.

Black and Marty follow us, with the muscle bringing up the rear. Once we are all outside and standing in a patch of slate by the back of the mansion, I glance at Marty. The muscle in his jaw twitches. Whether it's from uncertainty or having his loyalty questioned, I don't know.

Vic steps in close to Marty. The Adam's apple in Marty's neck bobs as the men stand eye to eye. Marty's back is rigid and his stare stoic which stands in contrast to Vic's lithe body and sleek movements.

Vic holds Marty's gaze as he slips a hand to Marty's waist. The touch is too intimate, too telling. Marty doesn't move as Vic's fingers linger before plucking the gun from the holster at Marty's waist. He hands it to one of his thugs before reaching for Marty again, this time provocatively undoing the belt at Marty's waist and then tossing it the other guard.

"Do I need to check further for weapons, Masterson? Not that I'd mind, but you already have an unfair advantage." Vic glances at me, his bald head shining under the spotlight that floods the yard. Vic thinks I'll trip on this, that I'll be too clouded to realize the truth and act on it. But I'm crystal clear on that account.

Marty is my enemy.

CHAPTER 3

I'm not blinded by emotion anymore. This little exercise is a means to an end. It gives me a chance to remove another obstacle from my path so that I can bring this entire house down and then I'll hold Sean again. I realize there's a disconnect there. If I bring the house down, the odds are that I'll be trapped inside. Maybe I don't need to touch Sean to say goodbye. Maybe I'll wake up in hell, and I can say hello. Good things don't happen to bad people, though. I can't count on that. I need to say goodbye now, while I'm out here.

Vic tips his head toward Black. "Search her for weapons."

Miss Black walks over, her cold stare meeting mine before she stops in front of me. Her lips form a straight red line as she lifts her hands and places them on my waist. Black runs her palms over me slowly, as if she enjoys touching my body and feeling the rise and fall of curvy flesh beneath her hand. That's when something odd happens. Her eyes are locked on mine when her hand goes right over the knife on my inner thigh. She caresses it and then sweeps past the blade as if it weren't there. She leans in close and brushes her lips to my ear, flicking out her tongue.

To everyone else, it looks like she's screwing with me, playing mind games. A curtain of silky black hair falls forward, and she breathes a word of warning, before pulling away. "Stab his calf and run to the trees."

I remain expressionless but wonder what the hell she has planned. When Black pulls away, she tucks the long strand of hair behind her ear, and I know that no one saw her whisper to me. They couldn't with those shining locks obscuring the view. I glare at her, wondering which side she's on. An answer rises in my mind. Black is on her side. She's always on her side. Which means if she's not Vic's ally, she's his enemy.

When Marty is stripped of his weapons and is standing in front of me, I lift my gaze. For a moment, I wonder if he's armed too— if Vic left a weapon on him the way Black left the knife on me. I wouldn't put it past him. My brother likes surprises.

Vic backs away from us as he spits out the rules. "I'd planned on killing her myself, Masterson, so if you don't make Avery's death a sight to be seen, an artistic display for me to witness, you'll be dead before her corpse hits the ground. You know how I prefer long, drawn out suffering. Amuse me, Masterson, and I'll never question your loyalty again."

Marty nods once, curtly, but doesn't speak. His eyes are locked on my face, jaw tense. Those long blonde eyelashes that once batted at me in laughter are attached to someone I don't know. The man wearing black fatigues is not the flamboyant gay joker he initially presented to me the first day we met. He's not the sweet man who held me while I cried. He's a motherfucking coward that's been hiding behind lies. He's always been looking out for himself, no matter what he said. Having no emotion to cloud my judgment makes things easier. Marty is one more obstacle to remove from my path.

Vic turns to me and lightly taps the palms of his hands together, grinning. "Little sister, there's no fucking way I'm letting you survive the night, but," he lifts a finger and then continues, "if you destroy Masterson, I might consider a brief reprieve. I'll postpone my previous plans for the evening."

I don't believe him. I ask flatly, "What's the catch?"

"No catch, you just have to kill him in a way that pleases me. Make a splendid scene of this spectacular body for me to admire. That's it." Vic's eyes rake over Marty like he's an object of desire. I wonder if Vic changed his plans for the night because he wants to do unspeakable things to Marty's dead body instead of mine.

I don't care. How is that possible? Apathy isn't impenetrable. There's a weak spot somewhere, and it'll sneak up on me from behind when I'm not expecting it. Can I trade Marty's life for my own? There it is, the truth. The act that promises me an existence beyond tonight. If I felt anger or rage, it'd be easier to accept this challenge, but I feel devoid of everything. Thoughts flow smoothly as I consider my options and weigh Black's suggestion against my desires.

The problem is that there's no vengeance flowing through my veins. I don't care that Marty betrayed me. His lies aren't eating away at me. There's no hatred rushing through me, making me want to do anything. Instead, I'm a walking corpse. I want to mourn, but there's nothing there—no tears, no tight throat, and no semblance of the person I'd been. Hollowness consumes me.

Black's eyes are on me, waiting for me to pull the knife, but I don't. I stand there wondering if I'd rather die than fight back. If that's the better choice. With no feelings to guide me, I don't know what I want. Emotions are what spur people to action, to fight back, to want to survive. At the moment, I don't want anything. No, that's not true. I chance a glance out of the corner of my eye, back to the pool with that bloody water.

Vic takes Black by the arm, which she dislikes. Her eyes narrow to thin slits and cut his face when she looks at him. She growls, "Do not touch me."

Vic chortles like she's funny. "Always playing hard to get, are we? Come along, Razelleia, my dear. We have prime seats on the terrace." Black's eyes flash with anger at the use of her first name. She went to great lengths to keep that information hidden, and Vic is flaunting that he knows her secrets—all of them.

Vic points to a stone overhang on the second floor. There's a wide sweeping staircase of gray stone that leads to the upper landing. Flower pots line the steps at the bottom, overflowing with blossoms. Black's heel connects with the stone, making a tap-tap sound as she climbs. Vic bounces up in front of her. Two guards follow them up, and two remain at the foot of the staircase.

Before Marty can do anything, I act. It's the only thing I want, and I don't care if it gives him an advantage. I need to see Sean. I race past Marty and move quickly, planting one foot in front of the other, taking long strides toward the pool. The grassy lawn rushes past, and I'm almost there. I have to see Sean's face. I need to say goodbye. The thought is covered in static, flickering like an old television screen. Everything will be fine once I do this. I can manage whatever comes if I have this moment. This fight is the first stepping stone on the path to the end.

Marty's voice is soft, urgent. "Where are you going?"

I ignore him and hurry toward the floating bodies, breaking out into a full run. I hear voices drifting in the wind from above and the sound of metal scraping stone as Vic and Black move chairs.

I'm near the shadows of the pool house, about to walk across a stone path when Marty catches up with me. He grabs my elbow and jerks me toward him and barks, "Stop."

His arm comes up around my neck while the other holds my waist tightly. His front is to my back, holding me firmly in place against his rock-hard body. I swing my arm backward and connect my elbow with his stomach. The impact is enough that he falters for a moment. I turn and look him in the face, in those brown eyes that were once so warm.

My hand hovers over the knife below the hem of my skirt, ready to pull it out and do whatever I have to do. I know where I'll aim and it won't be his leg. Mel showed me, taught me where to strike to take someone out. If I do this, if I take a swing at Marty, I have to mean it. I can't flash a weapon and then not use it. He'll take it from me, and I won't be able to stop him.

I glare at him. "Fuck off."

Marty grabs my wrist as I turn toward Sean's body again. I barely take a step when he hisses, "Listen. We have no time—"

I stop suddenly and turn, cutting him off, "Stop."

Marty glances up at the balcony. Vic screams to his men to flush us out of the shadows by the pool house. Marty speaks quickly, grabbing me by the shoulders, "Avery, please—"

Vic is bellowing into the night, "You stupid fuckers. You can't hide, and once they flush you out, you better fight or I won't be so nice!" Vic is hanging over the edge of the stone railing. I can see him from the corner of the house. He can see us, but the shadows are still obscuring Marty.

~ 25 ~

"There are no excuses for what you've done," I hiss. Vic's men are coming, and if they get hold of me, this is over. I raise my knee to Marty's nuts. He staggers back into the light, away from the edge of the tiny house.

There's a slow clap from the balcony, and Vic crows with delight before he yells out, "Do it again! Castrate the motherfucker! Come on, Sis. Show that bastard what happens when you fuck with a Campone."

Marty breathes, still bent at the waist. "Stay away from the pool. Go to the woods. Convincingly take me down and run to the trees."

That was an odd thing to say. Distracted, I glance at the tree line and then back at Marty just as he rushes me. I'm knocked to the ground and land on my back, skidding across the grass. Asshole. Stop underestimating him!

The air rushes out of my lungs as I collide with the ground. My shoulder scrapes the corner of a stone. The large pieces of slate have rough edges nestled in the pale sand that forms a pleasantly curving path between the pool and the little house. My skin rips open, but I can hardly feel it. Red ribbons of blood flow down my pale arm and drip onto the grass.

Vic is clapping and shouting obscenities. There are no neighboring houses in earshot. Why run to the tree line? Black said the same thing. It's not like I can jump the fence and get the hell out of here. What are they talking about?

I don't have time to consider it. Another floodlight turns on, momentarily blinding Marty. I twist out from under him, and when he reaches for me, I grab a fist full of sand from between the rocks and throw it in his eyes. Marty swears and backs off, rubbing at his face, trying to get the sand out. He staggers to his feet.

A fist connects with my side before I can decide if Black and Marty are on the same team. Marty grabs me by the waist and growls as he throws me down. I fight back. I don't know what I'm doing. I don't think or plan, I act coldly and hit his weak spots. A shot to his nose with a backward blow of my elbow spatters blood across his cheek. I use that bone in my arm as if it were a weapon, hitting him the face, then the chest until Marty staggers back enough for me to go for the blade.

When I slip my fingers around the cold steel, Marty is there again, his arms wrapping around me, trying to pin me to the ground. My fingers are pulling the weapon out when his head butts against mine. The knife falls from my grip and bounces into the grass out of reach. I slam my hand against the ground, searching for it.

Marty is speaking frantically, as he pulls my hair, his face contorted with rage, "Avery—"

My hand lands on something cold. I pluck it from the earth, making Marty stop mid-sentence, and swing. When the blade connects, he gasps and staggers back. When Marty looks down at his wound, and then at the hilt of the blade still in my hand, his lips part. The weapon is still in Marty's side as his hot blood pours over my skin. The powerful man suddenly weakens, falling to his knees beside me. His face crumples as he tries to regain his footing, but can't.

Those dark eyes look up at me. "I'm sorry. For everything. Get the hell out of here."

CHAPTER 4

Mercy swells from within me. Conflicting memories slam together in my mind—the way Marty defended me, saved me from the car crash and hid me on Oak Island. Those were lies; deceit intended to throw me off. It worked. I never knew which side he was playing for but now I know—it was for Vic.

My plan to leave Marty bleeding out on the lawn crumples and I throw it away. Instead of walking away, I crouch next to him and get down close to his face. I put my hand on his wound and press. Marty falls to the ground and howls. An eerily chipper version of the screech echoes from the balcony.

Vic is leaning back in his chaise lounge and slaps Black on the shoulder. "I told you she was a nasty little cunt. And you didn't think she had it in her." Vic grunts and then folds his arms across his chest and cranes his neck forward to see what's next. He cups his hands to his mouth as if I couldn't hear him and shouts, "Make me proud, Sis!"

My life for Marty's. I'll see the sunrise and he won't. If I live that long, I'll have an opportunity to free Mel. I need to know where they took her. I spit the words out between my teeth, "Where is Mel? Did you kill her too?"

Between gasps of pain, he breathes, "No. You need to run for the trees. Mel can take care of herself. Please, Avery. Listen to me. If you can get to the trees, you'll be safe."

Liar. I stand and pull away from him. Marty is curled on his side, cradling the wound. Looking down at him, I remember pancakes, stories, and those larger than life costumes. Which version of Marty is real? Does it matter?

Standing over him, I hiss, "Everything about you is a lie. Why should I believe you now?"

"Because I traded my life for yours." Marty closes his eyes as his jaw clenches tight, trying to endure the pain. "Finish this and get the fuck out of here."

Finish this? He wants me to kill him? That was the deal, my life for his. This is the second time he's said it, told me to take his life.

Marty doesn't look at me. His eyes are shut tight as he grapples with the pain. "Fuck, Avery. Even if you don't believe me, stay away from the pool and kill me."

I watch him writhe for a moment and confess, "I didn't twist the knife." Mel told me that it would do more than make a man fall. It would bleed faster, and the assailant would be nearly impossible to save. I had the chance. I could have done it, but I didn't.

Marty's eyes flash open, pure fear shining back at me. "Avery, please. Don't leave me like this. End it before it's too late..." His voice fades to a whisper as he grits his teeth to keep from crying out.

The moment passes too quickly. I never heard Vic approach. He is there, flanked by two thick men with necks like tree trunks. They have no expression on their faces, and their eyes are dead. Marty glances up at me, then his eyes land on Vic. Terror fills them in an instant. I can't do this to Marty, but before I have the opportunity, Vic is here. His movement and all its gusto make me think he's happy, that he'll give Marty a chance.

I don't see it coming. Vic swoops down, and there's a flash of silver as he swipes a blade across Marty's stomach. There's a deafening scream followed by the sound of Vic's crowing. He leans down and whispers something to Marty that I can't hear. Marty writhes on the ground, his hands trying to hold his torso together, but failing. Blood is everywhere, pouring from Marty's prone body and staining the stone.

Marty's face is white and covered in beads of sweat. With every panting breath, agony sweeps across his features. He meets my gaze for half a moment, and I swear that I can still hear his voice, begging me to kill him. The knife is still in my palm.

Vic kicks Marty in the side before standing erect and placing his hands behind his back. Rising up on the balls of his feet, gleefully, he preens, "Although I applaud your method of a slow, painful death, no one has that kind of time, dear sister. That would have taken days where as a stomach wound like this," he shrugs and glances aside, looking at the mansion, "he'll be dead in a matter of hours. It's long enough to think about what a dumb fuck he's been."

A cold void wraps around me like a blanket. I should care. I should be horrified. Instead, I'm drowning in logic, remembering everything the man dying at my feet has done for me. Whether I like it or not, I owe him a favor. This action constitutes a repayment even though it's despicable.

Vic senses my coldness and admires it. His approving look lingers on me before he claps his hands together as if ticking off another thing on his to-do list.

Forgiveness is foreign to me, but the methodical nature of courtesy is singing in my mind. I owe Marty. I can't leave him in agony, not when I can stop it. The movement is so quick, so unexpected that no one stops me. I lunge, knife ready, firm in my grip and slice Marty's neck ear to ear. I'm sprayed with hot blood as more of it leaks from his pale neck. His eyes meet mine one last time before they see no more.

I stand over Marty, holding his lifeless stare. I know I have a knife in my hand and that I did this to him. I know his blood covers my forearm and is splattered across my chest, but I can't feel it. There's a difference between knowing and feeling. I can't look away even though Marty is gone.

There's complete silence. Vic glares at me, fists clenching and unclenching. I ruined his fun. Good. He's a sick fucker.

The man lying at my feet is gone. I'm the one who took his life. A favor for a favor. How could I be so cold? Why didn't this tear me apart inside?

Because there's nothing left of you, a sharp voice should answer, but my only response is more silence. There's no consciousness telling me to feel guilt, shame, or sorrow. That part of me is horrifically absent.

Vic's face is turning red as he stands there, seething with his jaw locked. His men are still frozen in place and waiting for a command.

I glance at the pool again. The water is calling to me, telling me something. It says that I need to look and see for myself. It tells me not to walk away. I start walking toward the pool. It's only a few paces away, and when I'm at the edge, I stare down at the brown haired man floating with his face in the crimson stained water.

Vic is behind me a moment later, suddenly placid again. The man needs better meds. He flips from seething hatred to chipper way too fast. Is that what's in store for me? I never knew my biological father. What if my fate is the same? If I manage to live through this, my future is already cast. There's no way to recover from the things I've done, from the woman I've become.

Vic's hand slips across my shoulder. He hums in my ear, "Black didn't think you had it in you. I said that bitch has more bite than that. I knew it." He sounds as if he's trying to convince himself that I didn't steal his toy. "I told you to destroy Masterson. You did. You abided by the rules of the game, even though…" His voice is so tight that it barely comes out. "I wanted the kill." The words are strained, they're all lies, but the deceit is so thick that I'm not sure he knows the truth anymore.

"You can't get everything you want." The words tumble out, and I could not care less about recourse. I'm not thinking of anything at the moment, except the man in the water.

Vic tightens his grip on my shoulder, digging his nails into my skin and tearing it. He hisses by my cheek, "It's going to be absolutely magnificent to break you."

His words sound like bees, his touch feels like feathers. I'm aware of the sensation that something is there. But it doesn't make me move. Nothing does. The words are a wash of dull droning until that one word penetrates my haze—break.

I turn toward him slowly, allowing his arm to fall off my shoulder. My mouth moves and words come out politely, passionlessly. "Break me?" A smile crawls across my face.

Vic smiles back and drops his hands to his sides. "Of course. That's the fun."

I laugh lightly, hollowly. "Do you not see it? Can you not tell that you've already done that? I feel nothing—not sorrow or pain. I've lost everything, but you still think there's more take. More to decimate. Look at me, Vic." I grab his cheeks in my bloody hands and make him look me in the eyes. My voice is deep, steady. There's no plea, no cowardice, no bravery. It's devoid of everything I once knew. "There's nothing left of me. I don't care what you do."

He leaves my hands on his face and grins playfully. "I doubt that."

I drop my hands to my sides and glance at the water again, and then back at my dead friend on the ground. This feels fake, like it's not happening to me. How long do I have before transforming into a person like Vic? I can see edges of his brokenness. The lines that once defined who he was and what he's become.

I'd rather die. The words tumble out because I don't care what he knows and it's the truth. "Killing me would be a mercy."

Vic hoots and steps away from me, genuinely amused. He presses his fingertips to his chest and confesses, "I'm not a merciful man, but you will die. I can promise you that. In the meantime, I have plans for you." He kicks Marty in the face, and there's a loud crack as his jaw shattered. He giggles and glances over at me. "I wanted to kick someone and feel bones crack tonight. That wasn't nearly satisfying enough."

I stand there, saying nothing, and do nothing. Marty is already gone.

Vic swears and wails his foot into Marty's body again. That flash of calm vaporizes. I ignore my brother as he loses his cool and wails on the lifeless body, slamming his foot into the corpse, hard. When that's not enough, Vic gets on the ground and starts punching. Blood and flesh splatter as he screams at Marty, blaming him for dying, for choosing me instead. Vic is lost in a wave of unchecked feelings.

While I have no emotion flowing through my veins, Vic has every last one. All his wires are crossing, arcing, and causing him momentary lapses in judgment—this is what makes people fear him. It's the lack of logic, the complete and total hatred he carries. When it's focused onto a single point, Vic is a terrifying man. But that emotion also blinds him, and it'll be his downfall. He'll never see it coming.

CHAPTER 5

Turning away, I fixate on the pool. There's not a single ripple on the surface of the water. It's like a sheet of glass. That's odd. Water should be flowing. The filter is off, and the copper scuppers that jut out from the blue tiled wall don't even drip. They had enough time to stop flowing and the line dried. Maybe there's no power?

I step closer and lean down to touch the water when Vic's guard grabs my arm. I jerk my body away from him and elbow the guy in the gut causing him to step off balance on the rim of the pool. The curved edge is slick, and the guy goes down, swearing until he hits the water. There's a crackling, snapping sound as the man cries out. His body stiffens and jerks as electricity sparks from him.

Vic stands there next to me, watching with morbid curiosity as the man dies before him. The crackling sound mingles with a scream that seems unending. Vic lifts his slick chin and sniffs the air, grinning at the burnt, soggy stench. When it stops, the man's body floats face up, eyes wide with all life drained from him.

Vic smirks and takes my hand, pulling me away. "Looks like those fuckers did something before they got shot." Vic snaps at a few guards that were hanging back. "Make sure nothing else was tampered with by those assholes." He leers at the bodies floating face-down, his brow crumpled.

I watch my brother's body inch closer to the edge of the pool, and just as he is about to crouch down, I take my shot. I lunge at him. My hands are outstretched, poised to hit his back just below the shoulders. I make contact with one hand, my palm slamming into his shoulder blade. His thugs rush toward us, but they're too late, too far from where we stand.

Vic's laughter turns vicious when my body collides with his. But I hit the wrong spot. Instead of my body knocking Vic off balance and into the electrified water, I only manage to shove one shoulder which makes him turn. There's nothing stopping me from falling forward into the pool. There's not enough counterforce to stop me. As Vic spins, I reach out for him, intending to pull him into a watery grave with me. My fingers find his forearm, and I hold on, trying to pull him down with me. Just before my head hits the water, he juts out his other arm. With the balance of a cat, my brother perches on the edge of the pool, holding my body in a graceful backward dip, my hair dangling just above the water.

Vic snorts through his nose. The sound sends every hair on my body to stand on end. Or maybe that's the current racing through the water below me. His eyes snap to mine, narrow and furious. "Cunning little bitch. You pretend you have no spine, all this time cowering behind Ferro, and then what—you plan to take it all for yourself? As if you didn't have enough already."

His fingers dig into my back, and my heart is pounding. I can feel. The sensations are muted to a hollow echo of what they should be, but hostility trickles through me in a sluggish dose. My ankle twitches as I think about lacing it around Vic's neck and pulling him down with me. Before I can move, his words sink in.

Why does he think I have money? I scoff, sneering at him. "Enough? To what? Live in a fucking box?" The irrational bastard doesn't make any sense.

Snarling, he replies, "Don't play stupid with me." His grip tightens as he lowers my head closer to the water. His balance is much better than I can manage, his center of gravity stabilized. This went wrong. My neck strains as I try to right myself without any luck.

I hiss back through gritted teeth, "I'm not playing, you dumbass. So enlighten me. Which of my massive fortunes are you referring to? The mountain of student loans I have to secure a career that I'll never start? Or the wonderful home I own—oh wait, I don't have a home! I've been living in the basement of the university all summer!"

Vic's vicious sneer fades as he stares at me. Something I said shocks him. His eyes dart to the side, at his thugs, as if he's thinking before returning to meet mine. He swallows hard, and his grip loosens. This is my moment. I have no idea what threw him off guard, but I'm not asking questions. I twist slightly, enough to swing my foot up— enough to throw our entangled forms off balance. Our center of gravity shifts, tipping us toward the water. It can't be stopped. He can flail, but we're still going over the rim. A satisfied smile snakes across my lips as Vic cries out.

There's a metallic sound of something clicking, and when we fall over the edge, there's no splash, no pain, no voltage coursing through my body. Instead, we fall onto something hard. Vic tumbles to one side, and I go to the other. We both land on a plastic-reinforced cover that is feeding out from the wall of the pool just below the coping.

Black snaps her fingers at the thugs and frowns at Vic. "Are we done here? I have better things to do." She holds up a tiny remote for the retractable pool cover and rolls her eyes.

Vic stands on the cover as it connects with the other side of the pool, covering the deadly water below. He glances at me, panting and pale. He's insane, but he doesn't have a death wish. I tense, ready to charge him, but the thugs grab my elbows and pull me off the cover. Vic watches me, dark brows knitting together as his large hand rubs his chin. He ignores Black, doesn't thank her, or behave as if he's now indebted to her. If anything, it's still as if he's holding something over her head, so why not let us fall? Why the hell did Black close the cover?

Vic snaps his fingers at his men, commanding, "Pull them out. I want to see Ferro's face."

"Finally." Miss Black sighs dramatically and steps forward, one pointy scarlet stiletto at a time. She drapes her arms across her chest and tilts a hip to the side. "By the way, your plans for this evening went to Hell, Vic. I'm bored." She snaps the last sentence at him.

Vic's men had been about to run to shut the power off to the pool and pull out the bodies. But with Miss Black barking at their boss, no one moves.

Vic turns toward her slowly, a playful expression on his face. He gingerly places his fingertips against his chest. "You're bored? Masterson is dead, and you're telling me this evening is what—?"

"You screwed up, Vic. Someone threw a few volts into that pool, and you never noticed. I'm not willing to be compromised like this. Your friend, Masterson, obviously had other loyalties. You fucked this up. I'm not going to risk staying here another second."

His hand clamps around her wrist. She glances at it before returning her sharp gaze to his eyes. "Are you seriously telling me that this fuck up was my fault, you calloused cunt?"

Black's eyes narrow to slits as she steps closer to him. They're nearly nose to nose. She yanks free and steps back. "What did you call me?"

"I'll say it again, old lady. You're a calloused cunt," he sniggers, "and honestly, that's the worst kind to have. Too much time on your back fucked you over, Black."

She's in his face, hands at her sides with ruby manicured fingers spread wide, screaming, "I owned this town until you screwed everything up, you domineering little shit. You're not half the man your father was or Masterson wouldn't have turned your pool into a death trap. No one betrayed your father. Ever."

A low growl emits from the back of Vic's throat. "Except Ferro. Everything comes down to that fucking asshole. He's the reason everything went to Hell, not me. If you're going to assign blame, pin it in the right place, you sadistic bitch. You've always had a blind spot for Sean. You're fucking over the rest of the world to spite him, and you know what—he didn't care. What he did care about is right here." He extends a hand toward me.

Black is still tense, ready to fight. Her lethal expression slices over to me, jaw tense. She spits the words out, "What do you want me to do with her?"

Vic rakes his eyes over my body, not concealing his intentions. He steps toward me and runs a finger along my neck while saying to Black, "Teach her a fucking lesson while I have fun with her cock-sucking boyfriend. He died too fast." Vic's eyes darken while he's looking at Sean's body.

"Don't you touch him." I find myself growling at Vic, but he doesn't even look at me. Instead, his thugs flank me and grab hold of my arms. I try to jerk free. "I said…Don't. Touch. Him."

Vic looks over at me. "Really? You're going to beg me not to defile your dead fuckbuddy? That's sad, little sis, but I don't mind hearing you beg."

Black sighs as she folds her arms over her chest. "I'm leaving."

"The hell you are!" Vic is in Black's face. "All the fun is about to start."

Black glances at Sean's body as the pool cover retracts into the wall. She seems to make a snap decision. "Give me free rein with her." She inclines her head toward me. "Tell your men, or I'm not staying." Black is fierce and unflinching when Vic turns his unpredictable attention her way.

"Free rein?" The anger sours before dissolving into a chuckle. He tucks his hands in the crooks of his arms and tips his head to the side. "Exactly what do you want to do to her?"

Miss Black averts her eyes, looking me over again before meeting his gaze head on. "You're not the only one who suffered because of this little piece of shit. Let me do what I do best." She purrs as she lifts a perfectly plucked dark brow at him with a sadistic grin. "It gives you time with Ferro while I see to this parasite. Don't worry. I'll keep her in working order for when you return. And I know you want my assistance later this evening so make it worth my while."

Damn. I glance at the far end of the property, wondering if I should run. It's too late now. There are too many men, too many guns. I'll get shot in the ass before I make it halfway across the lawn. Plus, there's no promise anyone is out there. Marty may have been telling the truth—that there is safety in the trees—but who the hell knows what Black is doing.

A devilish grin seeps from the corners of his lips, and he laughs malevolently. "You earned your keep today, Black, as well as a bonus." Vic glances at me and considers it for a moment before turning back to Black.

"I want Miss Stanz. Free rein. Give it." Her clipped words are authoritative, and Vic looks pissed when she talks that way, but he doesn't laugh it off this time.

Instead, his hand is on his chin, and his eyes are thoughtful. He strokes his jaw as he stares at me. When he drops his hand, he nods to Black. "Do what you want with her, just keep her alive. But," he lowers his voice and steps into Black's space, meeting her glare head on, "you need to make it explicitly clear that no one fucks with me. Make sure she gets that. Make her scream. Use a hot poker on the bitch if you have to." He lifts a finger and adds, "Oh, and you better fucking record it."

Black smiles broadly. "With pleasure."

Vic pecks a kiss on Black's cheek before turning away. Somehow she doesn't stiffen or pull away, although I can tell that she abhors him. Vic looks me over. "I'll be back to finish her by morning. This ends tonight."

CHAPTER 6

Holy shit. This went catastrophically wrong. What the hell is between Black and Vic? What was that? Before I can decide what I witnessed, I'm hauled back toward the mansion by a thug. Black leads the way, sauntering across the lawn like she's at a picnic. Her shoulders are squared and she lifts her chin ever so slightly. Black hair is tied loosely at the base of her neck, allowing for strands to come free if not tightly tucked behind her ear. The waning moon reflects on her inky locks almost making them appear blue in the darkness.

Her red ensemble is impeccable and helps sustain her couldn't-care-less appearance. There's only a single cue, a tiny movement of agitation that gives her away. She taps her index finger on her thigh as we walk. Everything about Black is calm power. The woman never has a hair out of place, but that finger twitches every few moments while the rest of her body is docile, pliant. The façade of calm control is cracking. When Sean gets like that, a few well-placed blows fracture the entire wall. I wonder what's on the other side of Black's glossy exterior, what secrets she's kept locked up for so long that she'd spew in anger, just to tell another living being.

I take a wild guess. Something to rattle Black, to show her that I see the fissures appearing and that it's only a matter of time. Clearing my throat, I toss a comment at Black's back. "You're in bed with the wrong people, aren't you? Sean wasn't supposed to end up dead, and now that he is—you don't know what to do."

Black's index and middle fingers tense on her left hand. She stretches all her fingers to hide it, but I already noticed. Her back tenses as she exhales in a slow controlled way. It makes her ribs stiffen and impairs her ability to expand her ribs again, preventing another breath.

I laugh and think of the most outlandish thing to say. "Did you think you'd end up with Sean? After all this time, you really believe you had a chance to—"

Black rounds on me, teeth bared and lets her hand fly. Her palm strikes my cheek hard. The sting shocks me into silence before she grabs the front of my dress and pulls me to her face, ignoring the blood and gore.

Black's nose touches mine as she hisses, "If you value your life, you'll stop talking right now."

I wrap my fingers around her hands and dig my nails into the meat of her palms. "I obviously don't care what happens to me, so let's get it out in the open. You fell for Sean, but he chose me instead. That had to suck." The corner of my mouth tips up, and I laugh in her face.

"You're an insignificant little pawn." She shakes me once, hard, and pushes me away from her like I'm trash. "Victor and I are a team. Make no mistake about that." She glances at the tree line again, looking past me. I have no doubt there is something in the trees, but I have no idea what. Black seems nervous on top of everything else. Sean is a sore spot. I'm not blind and seeing him dead in the water screwed with her too even though she tries to hide it.

Black snaps her fingers to address the tall thug to my side. "Drop back."

The man is an ape, with hairy forearms the size of a Christmas ham. He shakes his large squared head. "Boss wants us to stay with her." He points a beefy finger at me.

Black rounds on him, narrows her gaze to thin slits and gets in his face, which is something since he's twice the width of her. "Yes, and your boss gave me free rein to do anything I like with this girl. I said, fall back. Challenge me again, and I'll make you wish you'd never been born."

The large man glances into the darkness that spans the shadowy paths back toward the pool. He lowers his head and holds out a palm, indicating we should walk ahead. He lingers behind us, following at a distance.

Black frowns and takes me by the elbow and tugs me forward. Her claws dig into my arm as she hastens her pace from casually slow to more of a businessman stride. Imagine Black with a briefcase on the sidewalk in Manhattan, except in this case she's striding on a carpet of grass, and I'm her attaché case.

Black moves with determined strides, spine straight, with her head tipped back slightly. While her poise screams business as usual, her voice does not.

She remains a few inches from my ear, staring straight ahead when she addresses me. "Play along, or we both die." It's barely a breath. There's no way the thug heard it.

I glance at her and look back at the man trailing us, suddenly wishing he were closer. Black is a crazy person. Not as bad as Vic, but in the same classification of sociopath with no conscious. "Yeah, sure. Anything you say, boss." I mock her and start to smirk.

Black immediately leans in and brushes her lip to my ear, speaking in quick hushed tones, "Just keep walking, and you sure as hell better not put up a fight." Her red lips linger there, and I stiffen.

Black hates me. I know that. So whatever she has planned is going to channel that hatred into something and aim it directly at me. She glances back at the thug, and her lips twist into a wicked grin of anticipation. As we approach the back glass doors to the home, she indicates I should pass over the threshold first and enter the mansion. I hesitate for a moment, meeting her eyes, wondering what she's doing. For a moment, I consider making a stand but think better of it.

After I pass through the glass doors, we continue down the hall. The thug doesn't follow. Instead, he remains in the vestibule by the entryway. Wine colored carpet stretches out in front of me as more gas lamps flicker, casting a warm glow on ornate wallpaper broken up by chunks of gold moldings, antiques, and paintings. We approach the far end of the corridor and a massive wooden door. Vic's man is still in sight when Black steps close. Her lean body rounds with animal-like speed and shoves me into the door. She presses her breasts to mine and lowers her thick lashes. I can't look away. I'm trapped between her body and the door. She warned me twice to play along. Is this what she's talking about? Why would it matter if she…?

Before I can finish the thought, her mouth is on mine, and her hand is my hair, commanding me—demanding that I kiss her back. She steals my breath as I tense in her hands. I can push her away and yell. I can try to overpower her, but Vic's man is only a few paces away, watching us.

Her mouth is hot, and she's strong. There's nothing shy about it. Not a second later, one hand holds my neck in place while the other slips down my side, and grabs the hem of my dress. Black slides her palm higher, making it disappear beneath the fabric of my dress.

Play along and then what? I can't think past that point because Black's tongue meets mine in a fiercely commanding kiss. I nearly jerk away, but she pulls me harder toward her. I could fight back now and have Vic's men restrain me, which will take away any chance I have, or I can wait and see how this plays out. People don't like public displays of affection. It makes normal passersby look away. Vic would probably stare, but he's not here—his guard is the one nearby, and the man appears extremely uncomfortable. He shifts his feet and avoids looking our way when Black kisses me.

Fight her. Fight him. Or wait and play the game in a way that is possible to win? Right now my odds suck. After a moment, I jerk away, slamming my head into the door. Black's hand flies and slaps my cheek before she clutches my face in her hand, leans in slowly, and then kisses me harder. The man remains where he is, his eyes bouncing around like a ball, jumping over us and then glancing at the floor. He looks back out the glass doors, shifts his weight, and then clears his throat.

What the hell is Black doing? I decide to do the only rational thing—I cave. The tension leaves my body. I clear my head and stop fighting her. Eyes closed, I pretend she's Sean. My hands cup her cheeks as I kiss her back, softly. She sighs in my mouth, and her arousal seems real, which confuses me. There's a brief moment when she pulls back and looks at me before she slams me into the door, pressing her body tighter to me until our curves line up flawlessly. It's odd, having this many breasts here. Before I can contemplate whether I'm excited by this or confused, the door opens.

Black must have opened the door. She extracts herself from me and inclines her head toward the empty room, indicating I should enter before turning back toward the thug. She arches a brow at him and gives a sadistic smile before following me into the space and closing the door.

Her fingers touch the corners of her mouth as her eyes rake over me. "That was rather convincing, but then again, so was your little stunt in the office. Are you considering changing teams, Miss Stanz?"

I keep my back to her, against my better judgment, and glance around the room. The lamps are off, and the only reason I can see the tall bookcases and velvety furniture is because of the pale beams of moonlight coming in through the windows. They cut through the darkness, casting the room in boxy shadows.

Still poking around, running the pads of my fingers over ancient books on a thick shelf, I toss over my shoulder. "As much as you are, I suspect."

When she doesn't respond, I turn on my heel and look at the woman. I hate her, but there's something there—something I almost comprehend. It's as if she's a mirror, a version of me a decade from now. I don't like what I see.

Black's hand drops to her side as she walks across to the couch and sits softly. She places one hand on her lap, before lifting the opposite arm and resting it on the sofa back. She glances over at me. "Tell me, Miss Stanz—Avery—exactly what do you suspect?"

"And spoil all the fun, Razelleia?" I lift a brow as I casually toss out her name, glaring at her, and fold my arms over my chest.

Black snorts and rolls her eyes. "You don't expect me just to tell you. That would be asinine."

"No," I correct, "That would be prudent, and if you're anything, you're always carefully prepared. But not this time." I pad over to the side of the couch and stand behind her, "Something threw you off your game tonight. No, not something, someone."

Black remains poised, but she's holding her breath. I know I'm on the right path, but my conclusion doesn't make any sense. Did she fall for me? Should I try and crack her or get the hell out of here? She managed to get us in a room alone. I need to know why, especially since she's made no move to assault me with the fireplace poker. There's no video camera as requested either, which makes me believe that Black has her plans.

As I ponder my next move, she replies with a lazy flick of her manicured hand. "We all have someone who makes us aspire to be more."

"No," I state firmly, "not you. You're a loner. You'd never side with anyone but yourself. You're just like—" Sean. I think it but don't say the word. Is that it? Is this about Sean or me? I stand at the end of the couch opposite her, arms folded across my chest and wait.

"Say it." She glances up at the dark fireplace. "I'm just like him. Just like your brother." Her dark gaze flicks up and latches onto mine, demanding that I meet her dark eyes. "You cannot offend me. Your insignificant observations cannot hurt me."

Black sits there, watching me carefully and radiating defiance. When she finally breaks her death-stare, she touches the golden keys that hang on the chain around her neck. She taps the one that has no diamonds, no intricate pattern, before working her jaw and resuming her former placid pose. Her crimson dress is still immaculate, unmarred. Unlike me. My black dress is torn and covered in Marty's blood. Bits of grass cling to the soft fabric. I don't brush the carnage off, and I don't cringe at the sins that are clinging to my skin. I pace a few steps away before circling back to her.

I redirect the conversation, trying to get at the core of this clusterfuck. "I never meant to do any of those things." For a moment I think I need to explain my meaning. But it's Black, and she somehow knows what I'm talking about—I see it in the somber expression on her face. She knows the dark things I've done, the unspeakable sins that should leave me cowering at the person I've become.

A moment of silence passes between us when Black barks a bitter laugh, shaking her head.

I step toward her and curb the sharp words that want to slash at the vile woman before me. Instead, I ask, "Is this funny? Then say it. Say you regret all of this. Say you made a big fucking mistake."

Her ruby red lips reply with a single word. "No."

"Really? You can stare death in the face and befriend psychotic assholes, but you can't admit how you feel about one man?"

Her dark eyes meet mine with a softness that disarms me. "Emotions are the Achilles' heel of life."

"That's very poetic, but it doesn't mean anything."

Black snaps, "Bullshit. It means everything. Emotions will lead you astray and ruin everything you've perfected. Then, when you least expect it, years after they've been buried and forgotten, a young girl will surface and bring those cancerous feelings back. It's as if they were never gone at all." She makes a bitter sound in the back of her throat as she lifts a hand to examine her nails. "Emotions become this colossal threat, constantly looming, and ready to break everything apart."

The sense of loss that fills the room is palpable. It's visible in Black's posture as she sighs and sinks back into the couch, pressing her manicured fingers to her temple. Hell, I can feel it, and I'm ninety-nine percent numb to everything. The hollowness of Black's eyes have a haunted expression that she rarely reveals, but at this moment it is completely unguarded. Her long tapered fingers touch the gold chain around her neck again, curling it around her forefinger.

She stares straight ahead, admitting flatly, "We die here, tonight—you and I. There's no way out. I'd hoped..." She trails off and shakes her head before dropping her hands to her lap with a thump.

I sit down at the other end of the couch, wanting more information. If the core of her statement is correct—there's no way out of this hell—then she's being held captive by Vic, too. I need to find out how.

CHAPTER 7

I slouch down into the cushions and pick the drying blood from under my nails, mainly to annoy Black. She'd smack a ruler onto my butt for my lack of perfect posture back when I first met her. Black was scary then. Now she just seems—lost. This is what's left after the tiger stops shredding everything and realizes it's trapped. There's no snarling, no sharp comments, or ruthless stares. She doesn't cower, but it's as if she knows her fate and it ends here. Just like mine.

If we have any chance of getting out of here, Black needs to snap out of it. I try to push her buttons and light her up. Teasing, I joke darkly, "What did you hope? To rule New York with Vic? Vic already has at least five lunatics living in his head. There's no room for another."

Black snorts. The sound is so unexpected that I glance over at her. Her gaze lowers to the couch. "If I had it all to do again, I'd make the same choices. The same mistakes. The things I regret are not for me, but for him—Sean. Then you showed up and..." She lifts her eyes and meets mine. "I hated you for it. You pulled him from that eternal darkness where I could not."

I can't look away. The pain etched across her face is pure. Her carefully constructed walls have disintegrated and blown away. There's no point in keeping them erected if she won't live to see daylight.

I can't help it. I half expect Black to be playing me but ask anyway, "Do you regret losing Sean?"

Her expression remains blank. "If I'd stayed with Sean, he wouldn't have been with Amanda. That train wreck would have never occurred." She takes a long slow breath as if pulling on a cigarette. She stares ahead, her eyes unfocused, her mind fixed on a point in the past.

After a moment the coldness in her gaze slithers back into place though her tone is far from calloused. "I accepted my lot in life, but I've never been able to accept Sean's."

The way she cradles her body forward, it's as if it's the only thing holding her in one piece. Sincerity is there in full force, and I finally realize what she's doing. This is a last confession. A tear rolls down her cheek, followed by another. She doesn't swat them away but leaves the little river of regret visible on her face. Remorse spills from her soul like I've never seen before—not from Black.

I don't know what to say. Black's tears are curious, so I sit quietly, watching her as if she were an aberration. I'm leery of Black and always have been, but I need to know how she went from the calculating bitch of business to the woman in front of me now. As far as I can tell, that disconnect with my feelings broke clean away. There's no fragment to cling to, to rebuild a bridge to my soul. That's the real question. If she's as I am now, soulless, how is she crying?

The abrupt change in demeanor makes me wonder if this is an act to lure me into something worse or if she's truly accepted this is the end.

Still leery, I regard her carefully, evaluating every movement, every breath. "So what changed?" The question is intentionally vague, allowing her to shovel her hole deeper or redeem herself.

Black lifts her chin to glare at me. There's a sheen in those dark, cold eyes. "You." Her mouth wraps around the word in a deliberate way. It's as if she were spitting out a disgusting piece of meat on the pavement.

"Me?" I ask, shocked. "What'd I have to do with anything?"

Her eyes lock on mine. "That's why this is so fucking troublesome. Vic wants you dead, and I'd kill you myself to get you out of the way, but—" She presses her lips together, locks her jaw, and cuts off the words. Her eyes close for a moment as she tips her chin to the side and shakes her head, brushing the traces of tears away.

"But you couldn't do that to Sean again." That's when I see it. She's truly in love with Sean. Her actions have been to protect him.

"Oh my God. This entire time—you were defying Vic and spared me for Sean. And then he died anyway?" My voice rises on the last part, making it come out like a question.

Black looks up at me from under her damp lashes as she sits forward, glaring with thinly veiled hatred. "It was all for him, everything I did." A smile breaks through and vanishes like the sun behind a cloud. "But it didn't matter. Sean was too far gone. Nothing I offered helped to ease his pain. There was no way to reclaim the past. Then you appeared on my doorstep, a serendipitous event indeed." She takes a long pull of air and leans back into the couch, her eyes raking my body before a menacing smile tugs at the corners of her mouth. "You could destroy me or free me from this nightmare. It all came down to you, and for the first time in my life, I was at a loss and didn't know how to proceed."

"It didn't seem like it."

As we've been talking, my posture changed from slouching to erect. Our bodies are mirroring each other. More head games from her, no doubt. I shift intentionally to see if she's trying to manipulate me into thinking we've similar struggles, but she doesn't move.

Despite her hard exterior, there's weakness penetrating the cracks of her withered soul. It's difficult to tell if she's breaking like I did or if there's a point past this, a lower threshold, something darker and deeper.

Black sneers. "Your Pollyanna naivety was amusing but short-lived. Stop pretending, Avery. This is your last confession, and most likely mine as well. If you have something to say, say it, or you may never have the chance."

I'm right. Black's clearing her conscience, trying to accept her fate with dignity. I don't know what I think about that.

"Fine," I blurt out. "I confess that I'm an idiot for not seeing sooner that you've had a target on my head since we met, and I suspect it goes back further than that. Does it? Why the hell was I singled out? Why'd you pick me?"

Black releases a rush of air from her nostrils before standing on those long, lean legs. She leans a hip against the side of the couch and folds her arms over her chest. "You're asking the wrong player. I'm not the chess master in this game. I got caught in the crossfire, same as you."

I try to meet her eyes, but she won't do it. Shock fills me as I realize that it's not defiance, but shame. I'm getting impatient, tired of being jerked around. "For once in your life, give me a straight answer. What the hell are you talking about?"

She crosses the room to look out the windows, her gaze on the trees and keeping her back to me. The moon casts a rim light around her figure, making the edges of the scarlet dress appear to burn. "Did you not wonder why Sean was at the corner of Deer Park Avenue, day after day? Why he was furious when you showed up at the restaurant as one of my girls the first time?" She laughs bitterly and turns to look me over, her face in a condescending sneer. "How could you be so obtuse as to not puzzle it out?"

The pieces were spinning in my mind for a long time, but then everything happened with Henry Thomas which snowballed into Vic chasing me down. I protest, "If one thing has been clear, it's that Sean is on my side. He's protecting me, so you're insinuating—"

She yells, her arms shooting from her sides, "Not Sean! Constance. Goddamnit, Avery." She snaps my name as if I were a dog. She turns to face me, her face revealing the frustration inside of her. "I was two steps ahead of Constance Ferro, right up until you walked into the picture. That woman has everyone in her pocket—except me. Not me. Never. I could run my business my way and do whatever I wanted. I was untouchable. The one thing that could bring me down, the one place where I was vulnerable, was Sean." The passion in her voice peaks mid-speech and then drops into a mournful wish by the time she utters the last word.

I stand and walk over to her, stopping a few paces away, still leaving a healthy distance between us. "What are you talking about?"

Black sniggers bitterly and then begins to pace in front of the window, hands flying as she speaks. "It was so simple, so brilliantly uncomplicated that I never saw it coming. I got a tip that you were tied to the mob. No one knew how or why, just that you were a prime bargaining piece. Several players made a move to capture you, but I won. I thought I was a genius using Sean to pull you in, but that's what Constance counted on—her son's involvement meant that I'd bend when pressed. Before long, my call girl empire turned rancid."

"Bullshit," I call her on it. "You knew you were selling women, kidnapping them, and enslaving them until they turned up dead. Don't pretend you didn't."

"I knew, and I looked the other way." Her tone is razor sharp. "Anything can be rationalized, Avery. A life for a life."

"You sold more than one woman. It wasn't a life for a life."

A deep growl rumbles from within her, tearing up her throat as she approaches me. Every muscle in her body is laced with unveiled tension, her dark eyes narrowed into thin slits. "It was never for me. It was always for him."

Black grabs my dress and jerks me toward her. I grab onto her hands, trying to tear her away, but Black's pupils are tiny. I swear to God. She doesn't see me even though she's looking right at me.

She sneers at me, speaking between clenched teeth. "I protected Sean as well as I could. When his mother disappeared, I knew we were all fucked. If someone defeated the chess master, then no one will be left standing." The tension drains from her body, and she releases me, her dark eyes meeting mine. "Constance Ferro was a force of nature."

Was a force of nature? Why is she lying? Black's either testing to see if I know Constance is alive or she doesn't know. I think back, and there's been no time that she referred to Constance in the present tense. It's always past tense.

I smooth my dress and shove her shoulder once. Not hard, just enough to get some tension out of my arms. Enough to distract her from my words, hoping she'll slip in the truth. "Yes, she was. I had the unfortunate occurrence of meeting her."

Black glances at me as if she didn't know, then nods. "I commanded my men to wait at the tree line on the far perimeter of the lawn, facing south. If you can get there, they'll take you to safety. There's no way out for me anyway. Once he finds out that I've been protecting you all along, I'm dead. Soon the pieces will fall into place, even in that deranged mind, and Vic will see everything."

My voice is stern, resolute, as I jab a finger to the carpet and lock eyes with Black. "I'm not running. This ends now."

There's a strange expression on Black's face, as if she's not truly seen me before. One of her brows lifts slightly, along with the side of her mouth. "There's no way out."

"Good, because I don't intend on leaving."

CHAPTER 8

With the little time we have left, Black and I both grudgingly share the plans we had to overthrow Vic tonight. We both failed. Black tagged along to make sure Vic went into the electrified pool, but something went wrong. Now she's here with a flawed extraction plan and too many paths that lead back to her hand in the attempt on Vic. That's why she grabbed the remote and closed the cover. There was no way Vic would get near the water after that. I tell her about our plans, which abruptly ended when Marty had Sean and Henry executed.

We're standing by the windows, looking down onto the darkened lawn below. Vic has yet to reappear, which is odd. Black expected him to return by now. Instead, there's a massive amount of swearing before the floodlights blink on below. The bodies lay next to the coping, covered. Vic is standing by the edge of the water berating his new head of security. The man stands there, stiff, as Vic screams at him. I supposed that man didn't expect a promotion when Marty died this evening.

We're in the middle of our conversation, but we both stop talking. We stare at the vast lawn, tall oaks, and sparkling water tinted red with blood. It's a strange sight. Black is straight-faced next to me watching the commotion below. Vic is a drama queen, throwing a fit when things don't work out exactly the way he wants.

Sean's death appears to have gummed up the works in Black's brain because she's silent, staring off like she's remembering something—or regretting it. I snap my fingers under her nose. "Focus. There's no time for that right now. If you can't concentrate, you'll get us killed."

Black's gaze becomes razor sharp again and slices me in half. "Do not lecture me."

"Then stop walking down memory lane. There's only one way to end this, and it requires access to the security room. I need your help, and I need Mel."

Her brow arches as she scoffs. "Melanie hasn't the comprehension nor the aptitude—"

I cut her off. "I don't have time to fight, and since you want to run to play another day, I'm telling you what I need." I tick off each request on my fingers. "First, find Mel and get her out. Second, make sure she knows we are on plan C. Third—"

Black cuts me off, "Mel's a liability. As soon as she's freed, Vic will know I did it, and then what? I'm tossed in a cage and sold with the others?"

Glaring at her, I snap, "You disgust me."

"Likewise." She narrows her eyes before ripping it away.

"Listen, this plan requires three people. Mel is the only one I'm certain will do her part. Marty is dead ..." Something clicks, albeit late, but it snaps into place all the same. "Marty told me to run for the trees. I need confirmation and not some bullshit answer— were you working with him or not?"

She sneers as if the mercenary were beneath her. "Certainly not. That parasite has been at Vic's side since before his father perished. If I'm not mistaken, and I'm not, they were childhood friends."

"What?" I hate having to say that, but this might make a huge difference. I don't have time to extract information from Black's head right now. Direct questions and short answers are needed since we're already on borrowed time. "Vic and Marty were childhood friends? Are you sure?"

Black gives me an 'oh please' look that infers I'm an imbecile for doubting her. "I'm one hundred percent certain of it."

"Then Vic betrayed his best friend?"

Black nods. "I suppose that's accurate."

"Why?" I look at her, hoping to God that she has infiltrated every aspect of Marty's life the way she has mine. She's like a fungus, seeping to every seam, every crevice, every corner of my life and just as toxic as black mold.

She laughs as if it were obvious. "You. Like I said, everything comes down to you. That idiot mercenary liked you. Anyone could see that. Vic didn't like it. The only thing I don't know is why your brother has fixated on you. He deemed you a threat and I have serious doubts it's related to jealousy."

I rub my fingers against my chin, my other hand rests on my stomach, unable to answer. Was Marty trying to protect Vic or me? Whose side was he on? Part of me thinks it no longer matters, but it might. Why did he tell me to run to the woods if he wasn't working with Black? What else is out there? I rifle back through our conversations and his behavior, unable to come to any conclusions.

Black's eyes dart between my hands. Her expression is stoic, cold, and closed down. Her eyes lock on the hand on my belly, and she puts the pieces together.

Her snapping voice pulls me out of my thoughts. "You cannot save that baby. There is no scenario in which that child survives."

Jaw locked, my throat tightens, as I lift my gaze to meet hers. Those are words that I didn't want to hear, that I can't accept. I'm polarized tonight. I'm willing to sacrifice myself, but not an innocent life—not a baby. I swallow hard, unable to reply.

Black's eyes look past me, her voice indifferent. "How could you be so utterly foolish? Do you have any idea what Vic will do if he finds out? That bastard will keep you alive just to rip the child from you at the last moment. Then, he will either sell it or play with it." She cringes when she says the last part.

I can't fathom what she's inferring, but Black has a picture in her mind. I'm sure of that. "What do you mean? Vic likes killing— it gives him a high. I've seen the look on his face."

Black's slender fingers knit together in front of her hips as she flattens her palms to her stomach. There's a tension in her neck that creeps down to her shoulders. Suddenly, she rounds on me, no longer concealing her thoughts.

She's in my face, snarling. "You haven't seen a goddamned thing to know what that man is capable of, what he can do. The greatest mercy you can show that child is to make sure it's never born so your brother can never touch it. And I see the wheels turning in your head—" She jabs a finger into my chest hard. "You can't escape him. Your mother tried to protect you, to hide you. Look where you ended up. After twenty years of running, you are standing where she started, in the same exact spot."

Although I knew all this, I failed to put in words. Somehow, speaking it makes it real, and even more impossible. I finally admit it out loud, "I can't save her."

Black drops her hand and shakes her head. "No, you can't. There's no way out of here and even if some miracle allows for you to live through the night—that baby will never be safe. It's the focus of everything Vic hates wrapped into one little package. Imagine if he took her from you? Imagine what that would do to the surviving Ferros? That baby is half Ferro and half Stanz—the two families he hates the most. I don't want to think about the existence that child would have, and the way it will die when Vic gets his hands on it."

As she speaks, waves of thought spiral inside my mind. I chase down one path of thought, and then another. Logic piles up and tumbles down—there's no way out— nowhere that we'll ever be safe. Black is right.

Even if we escape, Vic will just find us again. This was supposed to be our last stand, and everything was thrown into this evening so that Vic wouldn't walk away, but with Sean dead, it's impossible. Black is right. There's no way out, no way to stop the onslaught of violence that's coming my way.

I turn my back to her.

"Avery, be logical," Black speaks urgently, still trying to convince me. "Surely you can see it—"

"Enough." I cut her off with a single word.

Black's hand lands on my shoulder and whirls me around. She's in my face, speaking in a hushed voice. "It's paramount that you see it yourself. I know you're tenacious and cunning, but—"

I meet her dark eyes and nod once. "I'm never letting Vic near this baby."

"Then say it!"

"What do you want to hear?" I press my fingers to my chest and hurl a fury of words at her. "That I know I can't save her? That I can't even save myself? I die here either way, so I'm choosing how I go out. Is that clear enough for you, Black? Vic'll never know about the baby, and I'm willing to do whatever it takes to end this. Now. No second thoughts. I've decided." My chest rises and falls rapidly as my pulse roars, deafeningly loud in my ears.

Black tips her chin back in approval. "You have my assistance."

I laugh in her face. "And why would I trust you?"

"Because I got you alone and didn't beat the shit out of you, no matter how much I'd like to bring you to your knees. I could have done whatever I wanted with you. If anything, Vic would have held me in higher regard." She's in my face, and her tone has a lethal quality that I admire. She makes an irritated sound in the back of her throat, backs off and glances around the room, frowning. "You're not wounded, and I didn't record anything, so you figure it out. Either way, I failed to make you bleed. Vic will notice that as soon as he sees you. I'm fucked."

I nod in agreement. "Yeah, you are."

"Well, then," she replies, sweeping her eyes over me as if she's reassessed everything and made a snap decision, "consider this a temporary alliance. What do you intend to do?"

This decision is a vital juncture. I either trust Black and we work together, or we both die. If she screws me over, I'm dead anyway. It's flawed logic, but her betrayal wouldn't change my fate tonight, while her loyalty could alter everything. I tell her what I need. "Free Mel and get Vic back inside this house. Then go and break the emergency shut off valve for the gas lines into the house."

"How am I supposed to do that?"

"You're a smart girl." I pat Black on the top of the head. Anger flashes in her eyes. She swats me away, and I grin. "Figure it out. Tell Mel that I'll meet her in the trees on the south lawn, at the far end of the property, and make sure she stays put."

"Very well, but for this plan to be properly executed, you'll need an earpiece which will be difficult to acquire. Without it, you won't know what's happening and will walk straight into one of Vic's men."

"I'm more concerned about that bear."

Black's expression darkens. "There is no device on the bear, no chip or collar to track it. The animal roams free as if it were a pet. If you see that beast, run. Don't wait for him to make the first move or he will have his jaws on your neck before you can scream." She shivers as if she's seen it happen before.

Black and I hammer out the rest of the details. She helps refine some of the weak parts of my plan and tells me the most vulnerable part of the house. Although it's believed to be the most secure, it's not. Vic is blind to it, thinking his security locks will protect him.

I listen carefully. This woman is no stranger to atrocious deeds, but this makes me wonder. "Why do you know this stuff?"

Black touches her fingers to her head as if she has a headache. "Because I have examined exit strategies for my personal safety. I know every inch of this house. This proposal is much sloppier work with far fewer preparations than the things I had planned, but if you can to get to the central point of the mansion—Vic's bed chambers— game over. You'll need this to get inside." She lifts the chain with the golden keys from her neck and removes the plainest one. She hands it to me before putting the jewelry back on.

"What is this?" I look at the piece of jewelry, remembering it from the nightstand in Black's house.

"It's the key to Vic's master bedroom. He doesn't trust anyone, so it's always locked. The door is comprised of a dual lock. You'll need that key to get in the suite. The second lock requires a code."

As I turn over the golden ornament in my fingers, I ask, "Do you know Vic's code?"

Black shakes her head. "No, he changes it too frequently. I had an alternate code added by the security company as a master override. He doesn't know I have it and I've not used it yet. It was a backup plan if everything else failed." Black fills me in on everything about that room, leaving nothing out. Every piece of the plan to destroy Vic Campone Jr. snaps firmly into place.

Eventually, the plan is fleshed out with enough latitude that one mistake won't mean failure. Contingencies are in place should Mel not be freed, Black gets taken out, and to deal with the security cameras. The only roaming unknown is that white bear. I'll be able to hear his claws clicking on the hardwood, but not on the carpets. It's a massive white animal on dark carpet. I should be able to see him coming.

There's only one thing left to say. Black folds her slender arms over her chest and spits it out with no candy coating. She's direct and to the point. "You die tonight, Avery. There's no way out once this plan is in motion. The person lighting the fire doesn't escape. Are you certain you can do this? If not, we're all caught and—"

I cut her off with a forward tip of my head, meeting her gaze head on. "We're doing this. I know the ramifications. I won't fail."

"You're not the woman I thought you were."

I snort and turn away, glancing at the door. Vic will show up at any time. He left the lawn and entered the house a few moments ago.

I click my tongue and point both index fingers at her. "Neither are you, you crazy bitch."

Black smiles in appreciation. "Takes one to know one. Avery…" She waits until I turn back and extends her hand toward me. She rarely uses my first name the way she has tonight. I focus on her fully. "Saying I appreciate your sacrifice is a massive understatement. I made a mistake of pinning you as naïve when we first met. No one will think that of you after this evening. They'll remember the fierce woman who went down fighting, the only one who was capable of killing Vic Campone Jr."

I don't require her respect to go through with this, but hearing her say those words makes me more determined. I grip her hand as a farewell gesture. Black shakes for a second before she pulls me in for a hug.

When she steps back, the emotion on her face fades swiftly. She clears her throat and says, "When Mel is in motion, I'll say a code word that you cannot mistake as anything else."

"Which will be?"

"Sparkly."

I smirk. "I've never heard you say that before."

"And you never will again." Black's eyes dip to my waist and then back to my face before giving one curt nod. "See you in hell, Miss Stanz."

"I'm already there, Miss Black."

Black laughs once, and there's a bit of joy in it. The corner of her mouth rises. "Indubitably. So let's do this."

I throw the first punch.

CHAPTER 9

By the time Vic's man shows up, Black has scratched my face open and struck my cheek in exactly the right place to send ribbons of black and blue up to my eye. She has bruises on her neck and scratches on her arms. While we did all this to make it look convincing, it may have been real to some extent.

A thug pries her off of me and slams her down into the couch. "Stay," he grunts to Black and then looks down at me.

I'm gasping for breath the way Black told me to. The bruising on my side should make them think she broke a rib and it's pierced my lung. When no gurgling begins, they'll know it's not that serious. Until then, they'll think I'm dying which will knock my jackass brother off balance.

Black rights herself, muttering, "I'm done with this little bitch. When Vic wants me, he knows where to find me."

The thug calls after her, "He wanted the kill, Black. You fucked him over! Get your ass back here."

Black strides out of the room, her head held high and she doesn't look back. She puts the plan in motion. Not surprisingly, she knew exactly how the Ferro mansion went up in blazes so quickly. It was teamwork, open flames, and strategically altered gas pipes. The only problem with this plan is that the person who ignites the estate gets blasted to pieces with it. Chalk it up to last second planning.

I've considered it every way, unraveled every scenario which leaves me alive until morning, and they all end the same way. I'm stalling the inevitable. Vic won't stop coming for me, and even Black doesn't know why. I'd rather die in an explosion than be slowly tortured and mutilated. That decision drives me, spurring me forward. Relying on Black is madness, but I believe her. With all emotion turned off, I sense she's almost like me, devoid of feeling, even apathy. But it's when she spoke of Sean, a strand of regret could be heard that keeps her tethered to her soul. I don't have that. I'd feel jealous if I did. In the place of envy, there is just a calm acceptance—she will see Sean avenged. Vic won't walk away tonight, which is all I want.

I hold my hands over my right rib and cry out and then gargle the saliva pooling at the back of my throat. The thug standing over me pales, ignoring Black as she walks away, and then swears under his breath. He's about to speak into his earpiece when I drive my knee up into his nuts. He falls to his knees, and I kick out hard. The man drops like a rock. Ninja shot to the skull, courtesy of Mel. Blood seeps from the fresh wound on his temple as I extract the earpiece from him. I place it in my ear, grab his keys, and his flashlight. Patting his waist, I feel for a gun but there isn't one. Where the hell is it? We don't have time for this. I'll have to manage without one. His body is too large to move, so I leave him where he fell, exiting swiftly and locking the door behind me.

No one is coming until Vic shows up or the thug regains consciousness. Vic thinks I'm getting beaten by Black and confined by the fallen guard. I suspect I have less than half an hour before someone notices the downed man. It doesn't matter. That's more than enough time.

I follow the directions that Black provided and head down the hall, taking my first right and a quick left. Behind a tapestry, there's a door that leads to janitorial storage. Once inside, I flick on the lights. Ignoring the chatter on the earpiece, I find what I'm seeking. A large pair of pliers fits in my grip. The only way this plan fails is if they shut off the main gas line to the house, which is why I need Black to help. There's no way I can move through this vast house, opening pipes and setting the fire that causes the explosion if I'm outside by the main shut off. She knows I'm not coming back, and I have no doubt that if Sean were alive, she'd be the one striking the match.

No wonder why Black is so insane when it comes to me. She thought I saved the man she couldn't redeem. All along I thought I could bring Sean back from those dark places, but there were only small flashes of him. I didn't understand until tonight that there is no way out of this hell. Sean said he loved me, but how did he feel it? I don't want to think about that right now, that maybe he didn't truly love me at all. Maybe he couldn't, and that was the problem. He kept trying to tell me that it wasn't possible, not for him. It's not that he lied to me when he said those three little words, but there's a difference between a cognition and a sensation. I'd thought he could feel love, but if he felt the way I do now—it's not likely.

Mel will disable the security team as originally planned, so they don't see anything unusual. Without the black bead, she'll have to do it the old fashioned way. I need to wait a few minutes before moving again. It'll be a lot easier if I can do this without worrying about cameras. At the same time, the earpiece will cut out temporarily while she's putting the cameras on a loop, so I'll be moving around blind until it's done.

I sit down on a barrel of solvent used to clean carpets and listen to Vic snarling over the earpiece. "Fan out and lock down.

They're here. Those motherfuckers are still here."

I've been only half listening to his unintelligible ranting, and it's not until that second that I begin to concentrate on what Vic is saying. "Report back in three minutes. I repeat, full lock down. Fucking do it!"

Men's voices chime in order, giving location, current status, and then confirmation of lockdown orders until they get to my personal thug. No response.

Vic's voice is livid when he snarls, "G7, you better fucking be dead. G8, report!"

The flow of voices continues until there's a crackle on the line, and a new voice, distinctly female, and completely confident. "G7 is a worthless excuse for a guard. I may have killed him." She sounds nonplused.

Vic snarls, "Black, you better know exactly where the fuck Avery is or so help me God—"

She cuts in, static separating the speakers, her voice smooth and confident. "I know exactly where your little bitch is and what she's doing. Your taste is lacking, Victor. She wasn't very good."

"You're just jealous. I know you. You won't be happy until you strip that motherfucker of everything, you conniving bitch."

I press the earpiece as if I didn't hear them correctly.

Black replies. "I will despise Sean Ferro until the day I die, and his suffering is the only patch of light in this abysmal existence. Let's just say it's my sparkly spot of mirth."

Holy shit. Black did it. Mel is free and in motion. I need to break the gas valve in this room and find the suite Black mentioned. This house has gas fixtures everywhere, ensuring that this place will end with a fireball.

CHAPTER 10

Vic's men report but find nothing. My brain is on autopilot. I don't think about Sean or mourning him. I don't ponder anything except finishing this and punishing my bastard of a brother. Maybe I'll go to hell. Maybe I don't care. For the first time in a long time, my thoughts are entirely clear. I don't feel pulled in two directions. For a moment, I wonder if my conscience died with my soul, and then shrug it off. What happens when people become so broken that they run unchecked without any sounding board for their actions? How do they know what's right and wrong? Does it matter? I should have studied philosophy instead of psychology. I never read any case studies about people this fucked up.

I walk down the main hallways, avoiding the servant's passageways because I'm certain they're filled with thugs. It's not as if the main corridors are deserted, but it's easier to move with floor to ceiling tapestries to disappear behind when I hear footfalls rapidly approaching. I wait with a woven canvas blocking me from sight. Most people don't look down.

The toe of my black heels pokes out from the edge of the tapestry as I press my back into the cold stone wall. More footfalls rush toward my hiding spot and then pass by me. In the dim light, I stare at the threads in front of me. They're mostly dark shades of purple and blue with blacks and grays. But there's this string of gold that bobs in and out of it, marking its design on the front, perfecting it. There's no way to distinguish the pattern from this side, no way to tell if the golden strand was obliterated, but it appears again further down. From this side, it looks as if that strand is insignificant, a tiny, shining thread on a massive dark canvas.

After the echoes of rushing feet fade, I slip out of my hiding place. My heart doesn't thunder in my chest. I almost wish it did. I look up at the piece of art hanging on the wall to see what part that gold strand plays. I don't see it at first because of the kaleidoscope of deep gemstone colors surrounding it, but then it pops out, nestled next to a shade of violet so dark that it's almost black. The golden thread runs in tandem with that dark color forming a brilliant fleur-de-lis. The gold wouldn't appear so bright without the vibrant color nestled next to it. It makes me wonder if I lightened Sean after all this time or he darkened me. Or maybe we stayed the same because people can't change. The fracture inside my soul won't mend. Somehow I know that. Even Sean couldn't touch it if he were here. I wish I could cry and grieve for everything I've lost, how I've failed and suffered—but there are no tears, no anguish.

I peek up at the sconces lining the halls. The flames are housed in glass containers. If I disable the safety and blow out that flame, then the gas will build in that little glass box until I set off the main explosion, sending it racing down this hall and ensuring it'll meet up with the supply closet. No one ever looks up, so they won't notice that I've tampered with them until it's too late.

But how do I get up there? The ceilings are over fourteen feet, and the light fixture is around ten feet off the ground. If I push into a room to find something to climb on, I risk someone seeing me. As it is, Mel must have gotten into the control room because a flock of men aren't headed this way with nets, and my earpiece has gone silent.

Think, Avery. There's a chair, which is too short, a sideboard table, which is too heavy. Further down the hall is a window with thick drapes and long tasseled cords. I wonder if they're attached. Only one way to find out. I rush to the alcove and confirm I'm alone before yanking on the silken rope. It's a little thicker than my finger, so not the kind of line you'd need to dock a boat, but it should work.

I head to the nearest fixture, smirk as I toss the cable up and over the swooping decorative neck of the lamp and grab the other side of the silken cord as it falls. I wrap it around my hand and tug hard, hoping the damn thing is actually anchored in the wall. The fixture doesn't budge.

"Ha! Assholes." I silently thank God that I learned to climb the rope in gym class and shimmy my way up to the light, flick open the pane of glass and blow out the flame. I'm looking down at the regulator and don't smell gas. Cocking my head, I inspect the space behind an ornamental fitting and find the safety shut off. A copper wire connects to another piece. I have no idea if I'm pulling the right part, but I use my fingers and tug. The thin wire snaps and the scent of natural gas fills my nose.

I close the glass panel and slide down the rope, managing not to rip the skin off my palms. My fingertip is a little raw from pulling the wire like that. I'll have to use the pliers next time. From the floor, there's a faint scent of gas but nothing alarming. Move faster. One per hallway between here and Vic's bedroom which sits above the central part of the house. If Vic's room blows, it'll cause a chain reaction that takes out both wings with it. The fire will rush from the center of the house to the ends, instantly engulfing the entire mansion. I hope Black does her part. If

Vic is on the lawn, then this isn't going to work. He must be in the house.

I've climbed the rope seven times already, and my arms are sore. More footfalls race toward me, but I'm already hanging from a light fixture. Damn. I'm ten feet up in a blood red corridor that would have made Henry drool. Black marble statues of Greek goddess-like figures stand on scrolled corbels with their heads nearly touching the ceiling. Paintings form a line below their feet. The light still flickers in front of me. I scan the walls and notice there are no tapestries this time.

Shit. Shit. Shit. Where to go? There's a chandelier hanging from a rotunda that connects the two hallways, but it's too far away. Voices draw nearer, so I do the only thing possible and go up higher. Directly above my head is one of those statues. I use the cording and lasso the thing and tug lightly. It rocks. Fuck. I carefully gather my rope again and try to hook it around the pedestal this time. I barely have time to grab the cord, knot it, and climb before Vic's men come around the corner.

I freeze. I'm dangling from a gold rope about twelve feet off the ground, suspended between a statue and a gas lamp slowly spinning. I cringe, waiting for someone to spot me. I'm not exactly inconspicuous. I'm like a fly dangling on a spider's web.

Four of Vic's men stop below me. The tallest of them swears, and mumbles, "We're looking for a fucking ghost."

Another man with dark skin nods in agreement. "The guy is dead."

"Then where the fuck is the body?" The third man growls. He has broad shoulders with blonde hair that is tied at the nape of his neck.

The fourth man is silent. His face is obscured by a black ball cap, his clothing covered in yard debris, and he's thicker through the middle. He pauses and looks down the hall behind them.

The blonde ponytail guy pivots slowly, examining the walls and swears. "Why are the cameras showing Vic in this hallway if he's not here?"

The tall man shrugs as Mr. Ball cap flicks his eyes upward. His gaze lands on me for a fraction of a second. Fuck, he's going to shoot me. Or worse, drag me back to a room to wait for Vic. For a moment nothing happens. I wait for a voice to call up and a finger to point my way and announce me to his comrades. But he doesn't do that. Instead, he turns the other way, moving down the hallway. The rest of the men follow.

What the hell was that? By the time I climb down, my hands are aching and raw. The rope cut into my palm from clinging there so long. It's not until I round the corner that I see him—Mr. Ball Cap is waiting for me.

Great, more people who want to fuck with me. I stop so swiftly that my skirt swishes at the top of my knees. I'm ready to lasso his neck with my tapestry decoration and strangle him if needed. I loop the rope in my palm, preparing to move when he spreads his hands apart and smirks. "Avery, really? You hid on the ceiling?"

I take a second look at his face. "Gabe?" I can barely believe it. "You came to help?" He nods, and before he has a moment to explain, I scold him, "You have to get out of here. The entire building is going to be nothing but a bonfire."

"When?" He glances at his watch.

"As soon as I reach the master suite on the fourth floor. I'm nearly there." Three more hallways, a back staircase, and then it's the first door on the left. It's positioned directly over the center of the house. If Mel saw to the west side of the house, the supply closet coupled with this wing should take this entire building down.

"How much time do I have? I need to move my men out, but we're scattered."

"Ten minutes, tops. Better make it five. I'm not waiting. As soon as I get there, I'm lighting it."

Gabe's expression softens, and he places his hand on my shoulder. His eyes sweep over me again, noticing the bruises, blood, and gore. "Avery, you don't have to be a martyr."

"I already am." I pull away and continue down the hall, tapping at my wrist as if I were wearing a watch. "Five minutes until ignition. Get them out."

"Avery, you'll heal. If you give yourself a chance…" He watches me as I turn the corner.

I wish I believed him.

CHAPTER 11

As I sprint up the final staircase, a faint noise catches my ear. It's something familiar and light—not footfalls or like hearing someone breathing. It's more unnerving than that. The sound is as gentle as fingernails on a chalkboard with a similar effect. The soft scrape of knives across the wood, gently scratching the floor below—or claws. The bear found me.

Once I reach the upper landing, I can hide, but right now I'm out in the open. There are three flights of stairs, and I'm dead center. If I run, it's possible that I could hide. But there have been corridors with no quickly accessible crannies to wedge into, and if it's one of Vic's men, that'd be a problem. The line of sight on the staircase sucks. Damn it. I'm still frozen halfway up the second flight of steps. What would Sean do? Something crazy. I'm getting pretty good at crazy. Actually, I think I'm legally insane at this point. The men in white jackets will come to fetch me if by some stroke of luck I manage to survive the night. I've killed my conscience, and I'm considering doing something completely nuts. At the same time, the animal trailing me won't see it coming. Crazy and me are BFFs right now. There is no tomorrow, no worries about an asylum.

Screw it. I need to kill a bear with pliers. It's not something they taught me in college, and I can't say I've Googled it before either.

After coming to an abrupt halt on the steps to the second landing, I grab the thick banister and spin on my heel. I risk a glance between the fat wooden rungs, but no one is standing there. No crazy-ass white bear with freaky pink eyes. If I peer out too far, I'll get shot in the face if it's a person. Part of me thinks that it could be a person trailing me, using the sound to rattle me. But it's much more likely that it's the bear. I'm sure I look like a lunatic, crouching by the banister, thinking about doing what I need to do, flashlight in one hand and a pair of pliers in the other.

The scratch is inching closer, rising up the staircase, passing the first landing. There's a slow slicing of wood that's muffled by carpet. The sound is similar to nails scraping across paper. It's a noise that has always made my hair stand on end and my stomach twist. Now, it does nothing to penetrate that part of me. No sound or slow stalking will put me over the top. I've already been there, done that. What's left isn't someone I want to know. I wish I had a knife, but trying to take the one taunting me might not be the best move. I can't overpower anyone. I have shock value and crazy on my side, and that's about it. How hard is it to startle a bear?

I crouch low, as I peer around the railing quickly. There are five steps between me and the bottom landing. That's it. I perch on the stairs and look at the pliers in my hand and its curved edges. A blow to the temple will stop anything. It'll be like driving a knife into its skull.

The magnitude of what's about to happen, once I get past the bear, lingers above me like mist. When it fully penetrates my mind, it'll be so much worse. I don't want to think about it. I can't think about it. But still. My main regret is the baby I carry in my body. I wish I could save her, but there's no way out. Even if we manage to escape, I know this story. I've lived it. My mother couldn't outrun them, and she couldn't save me. All that's happened seems like a dream gone horribly wrong. I wish I could wake up. I wish I could strike a match and begin again, but I can't. There's nothing left to save, no soul, no laughter, no anything.

Surviving tonight would give my child the worst mother imaginable. Without emotion, without feeling, how would I love her? She'd grow up with me broken and half mad. That's no life to offer anyone. The least cruel thing to do is make sure I don't survive the explosion and take her away from here. That should sound awful, but it doesn't. She'd end up like me, deranged and running for her life with no sense of safety, security, or self. Her dreams would shatter and die when her heart breaks, when she realizes the world she's been born into, and the sins she has to repay aren't her own.

The slide of claws across wood abruptly stops, and silence falls around me. I'm snapped out of my internal debate on whether or not I'm cruel for wanting my child to never experience this nightmare. I'm utterly still, pressing my back to the banister, hidden by the thick post. I don't dare glance around the balustrade now.

He's there—I sense him. I tighten my grip on the pair of pliers. I have one shot at this. The way I figure it, I need to be airborne before the bear sees me coming. I have no gun, and if I throw my pliers and miss, I'm screwed. I can't hesitate, or he'll drag me back to Vic, half eaten. I'm not going back. I won't die like that, by Vic, or deranged bear. Tonight, I call the shots, and there's no way I'm fucking this up. The beast on the staircase won't know what hit him.

I shift my balance, still squatting close to the carpet, and prepare to spring forward. Everything clicks into slow motion. The pressure on the ball of my foot, my slick palm against the railing for support, and the tightness fading from my muscles as I uncoil. The crouch becomes the perfect assault. When I'm mid-launch a dark figure dressed in black comes into my line of sight. No white bear. This is a person.

Two problems instantly materialize. The first issue, I was counting on that massive bear body being substantial enough to break my momentum and keep me from crashing head first into the wall. The second issue, this guy isn't big enough to slow me down either. He's short. And curvy. The figure doesn't have broad shoulders, and his waist is trim, narrow. His hips flare into tight black pants with dark skin. I've got my tool held high, ready to strike when there's a flash of gold in a perfect circle by the dude's ear.

My brain put the thoughts into flashcard form, rapidly flipping through big hair, golden eyes, and a foul mouth that expresses displeasure by growling at me. "Awh, shit!"

I slam into Mel with full force. Her knife is thrown from her hand when we collide into the wall. There's a tangle of hair, limbs, and curses as she comes to a stop. Rolling, I hit the wall and flop backward like a rag doll with my neck hanging over the top step. I stare at the ceiling for a moment and suspect that my femur broke through my skin. My leg isn't at the best angle, but I can move it. I swing it under me and roll over quickly, making sure it's her.

Mel is sitting up, feet in front of her, dazed. The wall behind her head is cracked, and white plaster dusts her dark hair. She blinks rapidly and presses her hand to her forehead, swearing softly. When she manages to focus on me, her frown turns into a repressed smile.

Then Mel snorts and cackles, "What the fuck are you doing? You flew through the air like a deranged primate on crack!" She laughs so hard that it makes her wince. She presses two fingers to her temple and then feels around to the back of her head. When she pulls her hand away, she inspects the pads of her fingers for blood. There is a small amount, like she ran her finger over a red magic marker.

I crawl over to her and put my back to the wall. I'm doing a mental inventory to determine what broke, if anything, when I blurt out, "I thought you were Vic's bear."

Mel makes a nasally noise, affirming that she's not a bear and I was wrong. "Who says

I sound like a two-ton bear? What kinda statement is that to make?"

I snort. "Yeah, as if screaming about getting hit by a primate is normal. Who says that?"

Mel closes her eyes and holds up a finger. "Goddamn it. Don't tell me. Don't say it—"

"You've been hanging out with Henry too much." I touch a finger to my temple because it feels wet and warm. When I pull my hand away, there's a red streak. I frown at the injury. "We shoulda 'shipped you two."

Mel shoots me a nasty look. "Don't you dare."

"Melry? Henel?" I snort and grin at her, "Oh, I've got it. Melry. Where's your better half anyway?" I stand and quickly remember exactly where Henry is—next to Sean, lifeless in the pool. Damn it, why did I ask that? He's dead. I knew that, and I forgot. My mind is so fucked up right now.

Mel gets up next to me with no expression of remorse, other than sounding like Henry. She doesn't comment on his location or whether or not she knows he's dead. She wasn't in the room at the end, so she probably doesn't know.

The earpiece became dislodged when I collided with the wall. I walk over and pick it up. It got trampled a bit but is still making noise. "I guess this thing is finally back online."

Mel smirks and stands. "Yeah, should be by now."

After putting the small electronic back in place, I listen. Most of the reports are static, but I can make out a few words. I swear and let out a rush of air, smearing the blood away from my eyes and wishing I had a way to make it stop dripping. "Head wounds bleed too much."

"No shit." Mel approaches, looking me over. "It'll be okay. A few stitches and you'll be good as new."

Not that it matters. I tug at the hem of my dress, pulling at the seam until it rips. With a firm tug, I rip off the bottom of the skirt and tie it around my head to slow the blood. It's not very absorbent, but it's enough to keep the wound from pouring into my eyes.

Mel watches me for a second and asks, "And don't think I didn't hear you. And it's not like we shouldn't talk about him. I mean, you see what you saw. So, tell me truly—you really think he's my better half?"

Her question shocks me. So she honestly doesn't know that Henry is dead. I make a garbled response, "I, ahhh—"

She cocks her head and makes an incredulous expression. Pressing her hand to her chest, she repeats, "Really? That sick, twisted man is better than all this?" She gestures to herself, hips to head, and offers an 'I didn't think so' smirk.

I snap my fingers in front of her face. "Focus." Then I flinch. Who does that? I hate it when someone does that to me.

Mel blinks like I've grown an extra face on my ass. "You did not just copy Black's insolent dog move on me. I swear to God, Avery, if you ever do that to me again I'll bite your goddamned finger off."

I look her full on, our eyes meeting and holding. "I hear you."

Those three words say it all: I understand. I'm sorry. I'm not going to be able to finish this conversation. There is no tomorrow for me.

Mel's movement is so swift and unexpected that I don't see it coming. All of a sudden her palm collides with my cheek.

The sting sinks in, the pain is far too light, feeling more like a butterfly kiss than a slap.

She narrows her tiger eyes and is all predator as she gets in my face. "No, you don't hear a goddamned thing. Why do you think I'm here? Avery, you're not doing this."

I look her in the eye and feel nothing, not regret, pain, or grief. Numbness consumes me. My brain is firing off different plans, running down different possibilities to get her out of here. She's going to insist on staying, but she shouldn't. She has a future. She'll fight to see the sunrise, but I'm done.

Mel sees the thoughts in my eyes and places her hands on my shoulders. I expect her to shake me and yell, but she doesn't. "Listen, I don't know fuck about anything, but I know what I see. A woman with no future who's ready to wipe out her past." She starts the walk down the final corridor, the long hallway that leads to the master suite in the middle of the mansion. "But why not try to get out? You gotta at least try, Avery."

My decision was calculated. I answer plainly, without an ounce of regret. "The only way to make sure it lights is to be in the room. The balcony window is too high to jump. A fireball will melt the skin off my back, and I'll break my neck in the fall. Besides, if I'm close enough to light it, then I'm close enough to die. I don't want to be far enough to live, but close enough to burn." I glance over at her.

Mel nods slowly. "My wing is done. They're going to smell it soon. Black headed out, last I saw. Even if she don't get the main line ready, this motherfucker is going to burn along with everyone in it. You won, Avery."

"It doesn't feel like it."

Mel nods in agreement. "So, let's go all Thelma and Louise on Vic's ass and end this. He's in the control room. I saw him. It's over as soon as you light the match."

I stop abruptly and take her hands tightly, pressing them beneath both of my palms. "I can't make you do anything, but I know you. You're a fighter. Even if you get torched in a backdraft, you won't die. Do you seriously want to live through this? Third degree burns, skin grafts, and deformity coupled with lifelong pain?"

She snorts and tries to pull her hands away, but I don't let her. "Mel, I'm serious. You've defied the odds since you were a kid. I just smashed a pair of pliers into your head and slammed you into the wall. I'm the one who's worse for wear, not you. I only scratched you."

"I've got a hard head. We both know that." She tries to lighten things, but I don't smile back at her.

"I'm serious. This won't kill you. Somehow you'll make it, but you sure as hell are going to wish you were dead if you're anywhere near me when I light this thing. Getting your entire body covered in third-degree burns isn't in your future." She doesn't argue. "Besides, someone needs to tell Henry's next of kin that he was a hero at the end. You can do that in a way no one else can. I wouldn't have believed it."

"Me neither. So Henry's gone, then? Dead?" she asks somberly, completely serious for once.

Nodding, I reply, "I'm afraid so."

She inhales sharply through her nose, eyes full, and presses her lips together before admitting, "Goes to show people aren't always as bad as you think. But I am. I never thought Black was up to her neck in this kinda shit. I wouldn't have done this to you. It's my fault."

"No, it's not." I catch her eyes. "I was already gone before this started. Even when I thought I had a chance, it's just not going to happen. Eventually, some people bleed out, Mel. There's nothing left to save."

She doesn't meet my gaze, doesn't nod, doesn't verbally tell me she agrees, but I know she does. I see it in the downward cast of her eyes, and the way certainty flickers across her features. It's a small ripple of acknowledgment across the vast lake of life.

She rounds on me and throws her arms around my shoulders, hugging me so tight she could crack a rib. "If you can get out, if there's any chance at all, take it." When she pulls away, her eyes are glassy, but those tears will never fall.

I nod and step back. "I will."

"Seriously, I can't leave you. How the fuck am I supposed to just walk away?"

There's a scrape of a floor board below followed by a deep grunt. Mel stiffens and backs away from the edge of the step. I do the same. We wait a moment and when the sound repeats Mel puts a finger to her lips. She edges toward the railing, peering straight down the center of the stairwell. Her amber eyes widen as her jaw drops. She jerks back, her finger still pointing below, unable to speak.

"What is it?" I whisper, but she just shakes her head. I carefully slink forward and look for the sight that rendered Mel silent. A great white bear is meandering up the flight below us. His haunches move, shifting his massive weight, as he takes one step at a time. The once white fur is matted with crimson along the side of his muzzle and down his side as if he's recently had someone in his maw.

I tip my head toward the upper landing, indicating we should move. Now. Mel follows in silence, hurrying down the long corridor that connects to the central staircase. It's out in the open and completely stupid to descend at this location, but there's a bear in the other direction, and from the look of him, that beast already ate someone tonight.

Mel finally speaks once there are a few hallways between us and the animal. Her voice raspy, as she points in the direction, we came. "That fucker has a bear? For real? I heard he had it, but who the hell has a pet bear? And his fur. Avery..." The shocked expression on her face doesn't fade as she puts her hand over her mouth.

"I know. Marty told me it was here. When I saw it earlier, that thing wasn't covered in blood."

"Great" Mel's voice cracks, "he ate someone."

"Take this way out. Avoid the damned bear."

Mel nods, still shocked. "Shit, Avery, I thought I'd seen everything. But now," she shakes her head, "shit. A bear." She smiles at me tentatively, through the fingers of the hand splayed across her face. She takes it away and looks me in the eyes. "I don't know if I can do this."

I speak with more confidence than I have. Saying goodbye sucks. "Just turn around and don't look back. You better go now before he sniffs us out." I turn away from her, so she doesn't have to, and walk away.

"Shit, girl." Mel's voice hitches. "Promise me. Say it. This wasn't for nothing."

"Psh," I smile at her over my shoulder, "none of this was for nothing. It works out in a master plan where the seriously evil dude gets his ass kicked by the naïve doe-eyed co-ed."

"The dumbass that pegged you as that chick is going to be sorry. I've always seen what you really are…"

I say over my shoulder, "I'll give you two minutes to get out. Hurry."

Mel nods tersely and rushes down the hall with the gracefulness of a feline. She glances back at me one last time. Then I'm alone.

CHAPTER 12

The massive double door entry to Vic's
master suite stands directly in front of me.
The doors are covered in black lacquer and
gleaming as if they've never been touched.
This location is in the central corridor that
connects the entire house on the upmost
floor. This is where everything ends. Once I
step over the threshold, my life ends. Black
warned me that there is no way down and no
way out. Since Henry is gone, there is no

fancy tech or drones to ignite this hellhole. It has to be me.

I square my shoulders and pull out the gold key. I slip it into the lock and twist. The copper keypad to the right illuminates and prompts me for a code. I copy it from the head of the key, pressing one digit at a time. If this is the wrong number, an alarm will go off. I won't get to stop Vic. This is the moment where I find out if Black was full of shit. After touching my finger to the pad for the final digit, I wait and stare at the terminal. The illumination on the box turns green and a second lock on the door clicks open. Black was telling the truth.

I put my palms to the smooth ebony door and push into the room. There's a small corridor directly inside the door that spills out into a vast cream room covered in slick marble. Gold leaf covers the barrel ceiling in tiny squares leading to the opulent picture window at the far end of the suite. There's a set of French doors standing partially opened. White gauzy curtains billow as the night breeze blows inside. The scent of vanilla fills my head as I flick my gaze around at the flickering gas fixtures. To my right is a bathroom with long marble counters. Tiny soaps in the shapes of enormous creamy pearls fill oversized vases that stretch from floor to ceiling, flanking the entry to the bathing area and creating the warm, sugary scent. To the right is a cavern of a room devoid of light. Murky carpet lines the floor and swallows the space in blackness. That must be the bedchamber. I walk the walls of the foyer once, gliding along the glossy floor, listening for Vic—making sure I'm alone.

There's not a soul here, but hairs on the back of my neck prickle as if I'm being watched. No sounds, no footfalls. I take another step into the space, silently padding into the middle of the grand bathroom. Multiple stalls are at one end with too many sinks at the other. I twist my wrist so I can see my watch. Mel needs another minute to haul her ass to safety.

The sensation of eyes on me doesn't fade. There are no cameras in here, unlike the lined hallways. I dodged Vic's men thanks to Mel. She randomly disabled cameras throughout the mansion, so no one saw me coming. Or maybe she took out the entire team in the security room; I don't know exactly how she did it. I didn't have time to ask, but there are no cameras in here so why do I feel like I'm being watched?

The breeze billows the hem of the curtains again, and I resist the urge to walk outside and look down at the pool below. Occasionally, Vic's voice crackles over my headset, angry. I only get bits and pieces of garbled ranting as more checkpoints respond. If he's in the security room, then he's reviewing footage and trying to determine what happened to his pool. Vic is paranoid and thinks enemies are everywhere.

Sean had told me that he was a monster, that he poisoned everything he touched. That truth is vivid now. With a freshly fractured spirit, I can see him for what he was— broken. People can still function if they retreat into themselves and never examine anything. But Sean wasn't like that. Amanda's death put him on a crash course with cruelty. He thought it turned him into a twisted excuse for human life, but it didn't. Sean went through the fire and survived. In those rare moments where he dropped his guard and didn't shut me out, I could see pure kindness behind his eyes. In a world that treated him so unkindly, any scrap of humanity should have died a long time ago. When I met Sean, he was giving into it, becoming the creature people accused him of being. I'll remember the man who sacrificed everything to save the ones he loves most—his brothers, his parents, and me. I know a monster when I see one, and my brother has learned to fill every aspect and play the part to walk with mortals, but he belongs in Hell.

While my mind wanders, I walk the room, checking the massive bathroom and bedchamber for signs of life, but there are none. Still, I can sense that there's someone here. The prickling sensation of an unseen glance caresses me over and over again. It's like standing in a gentle breeze which is equally invisible but real. I pad into the murky master suit and stride directly over to a set of double doors that lead to a huge closet. I yank them open, expecting to come face to face to with a person. I'm not certain who, but no one is there. Damn it. I'm certain about this. Someone else is here. I may not feel a goddamned thing, but my Spidey-sense is going batshit crazy. Eyes are on me, watching me, waiting in silence.

I back toward the massive foyer and stand in the center of the ivory colored room.

Tipping my chin up, I speak into the air, "I know you're here. Show yourself."

I back toward the doors into the hallway and flick the big bolt, locking the door. No one will be able to enter the room unless they have a bulldozer. I tighten my grip on the pliers and press my other palm to the light switches and break the circuit. The overhead electric lights go dark, but the room isn't pitch black because of the gas lamps. The flames flicker in front of the wall of mirrors, painting the entry room in a golden hue.

Raising the pliers higher, holding them in line with my heart and ready to strike, I slowly circle the room. It's not until the wind blows the silken fabric for the third time that I consider the balcony. The hairs on my arms rise as I take a step toward the French doors. As the drapes shift in the breeze, I can make out the silhouette of a figure seated in a chair toward the very edge of the stone terrace. My eyes haven't adjusted enough to the dim light to see his face, but his back is toward me. Did Vic get up here before me? Why is he sitting? Is this Vic's way of playing with me?

The urge to run sears through my legs and makes my heart pound. I could run forward and crash my pliers into the side of his head, or stay where I am and light this place up as soon as I remove the safety on the light fixture. Calm nerves, thick and steady like thick ropes from a ship, overtake my arms and legs. I find my resolve and don't frantically do anything. If this is Vic, he'll die with me in this fiery hell. I refuse to divert from my plan.

There's a light fixture to my left, flickering beautifully, waiting for me. I'll get to the asshole waiting for me, but first I'm doing what I came here to do. Vic can laugh in my face and torment me as much as he wants. It will only last a split second before I blow this place to hell.

As I pad toward the gas lamp on the wall, I don't turn my back to the figure on the balcony. I know he sees me. I'm not the one making the first move or saying the first word. Fuck him. Two can play this game. There's no reason to talk, nothing to say that can destroy me any more than he already has.

I crash the pliers into the glass housing surrounding the light fixture, breaking it. Shards fall to the floor in a cascade of noise. There's no reason to be quiet. Vic knows I'm here. By the time he figures out what I've done, he'll get eaten by a fireball.

Turing my attention back to the lamp, I examine it quickly. The flame is exposed, and before I do anything else, I take the metal tool and slam it into the coupler housing the safety shut off. The tiny wire can't take the hit, and it wasn't designed to. The telltale sound of gas rushing through pipes fills my ears as the sulfuric scent fills my head. I pull a lighter from my other pocket, walking slowly toward my twisted sibling.

A smile tugs at my mouth. There's no way out. If he jumps, he's dead. If he stays here, he's dead.

I start talking, saying whatever comes to mind. "I never knew why Mom was always so afraid. I mean, I sensed it—that something happened to her when she was younger—but I never thought it was this. I never thought your sonuvabitch father touched her. She lived in fear for over twenty years, constantly looking over her shoulder, trying to protect me—trying to save us."

A deep sadistic laugh is my only answer.

"You know," I press forward, rubbing my thumb against the side of the lighter as I walk, "I always wanted a brother, any family actually. I'd dream about those big family holidays with tons of cousins and aunts and uncles. A place where we belonged, with people who loved us. Instead, I got you, you sick, fucking sadistic lunatic."

"That's terrible," Vic says from the balcony. His voice carries oddly through the space, almost as if it's coming from behind me. I look back, but the room is empty. He's on the balcony. I can see him, sitting there, smugly slouched forward toward the rail. Sick fucker. Maybe the vast marble room bounces sound in weird ways. Either that or I've had one too many shots to the head tonight. Both theories are entirely possible.

"Well, guess what?" After one more step, I stop. I need to lure him back inside just to be certain he dies. The balcony is second choice and better than nothing. Still, I can make him come to me. His arrogance is too enormous to sit there and do nothing. I smirk and hold up my hand with the lighter high above my head and call out, "The Campone line ends with us! There's no way out. I'm the death angel, and it's time to pay for everything you've ever done. If I burn for eternity because of it, so be it. It'll be worth it to make sure you're erased."

No reaction. Vic just sits there like he's at a fucking picnic. He doesn't move or speak.

I pause for a second, considering grabbing Vic and dragging him back into the room. Every inch of my body is corded tight, ready to fight. The one thing I can't account for is the swirling in the pit of my stomach. I went from feeling nothing to that queasy sensation when I passed over the threshold. It's still there even though I heard Vic's voice. Maybe it's gas poisoning? I already inhaled too many fumes for one night.

There's a nudging at the back of my mind that won't leave it alone. I debate the need to see Vic's face, to watch his eyes as I end us, but that creates more risk. Still, my eyes sweep over the form, the stance, and won't stop picking at the wrongness of it, but there's a massive amount of shit wrong with Vic. I always react this way around him. My skin prickles more and more until every inch of my body is standing on end. Screw it. There's enough gas seeping out into the night air that I can light this motherfucker up and end it. Decision made. Done. I'll step onto the terrace and flick the lighter, and we'll both be swallowed in a cloud of flames. Resolve pumps through my veins as I shove through the sheer fluttering fabric and out onto the stone verandah.

I lift the lighter ready to flick it, thumb already increasing pressure. All I need is a downward thrust of my thumb, and this is over. That's when I come face to face with someone I never expected to see again.

The form in front of me isn't Vic. It's a woman, hunched forward, head down. Her hair is matted and clumped to her skull. The once full figure is frail and beaten, but I'd know her anywhere.

"Mom?"

CHAPTER 13

My voice cracks as my eyes sweep over her emaciated body. Her once smooth skin is covered in grime, old wounds, and dried blood. The skin hangs off her bones as if she's not had enough to eat in months. I forget everything in those seconds, the lighter, the sick bastard still in the room—all of my attention is on the woman facing away from me in that chair.

It can't be Mom. There's no way. I saw her dead body...wait. No, that's not true. I didn't. I saw Daddy's twisted lifeless form and refused to look under Mom's sheet at the morgue. I saw her feet poking out from beneath the cloth. I wasn't the one who identified my mother. The doctor did—said it was her—that they were together. They left the house together. They went to get ice cream. I was supposed to be there. The memories drown me in a deluge of rapidly firing images and voices that sound like clipped recordings.

A scream lodges in my throat, choking me. There's no air. I stagger back a step. This can't be. It's possible it's someone else. The only way to be certain is to step to the side and see her face. It's not her. There's no way. I inch over and gape at her profile. My gaze sweeps over the curve of her cheek and the sunken eyes. A single birthmark is on her neck, just above her collarbone. A memory surfaces of an eight-year-old Avery wrapping her arms around Mom's neck—seeing that mark. She smelled like vanilla and summer flowers. The perfect mixture of warmth and sunshine.

The scent of the room hits me like a hammer to the face. It's nostalgic, intentionally. Vic planned this. He did it on purpose. That's my mother's perfume filling the air.

The woman in the chair, the woman with my mother's face and withered body slowly lifts her head. When our eyes meet her features crumple in horror. "Avery?"

Her voice is a dry husk of what I remember. Is it her?

Wide-eyed, I gape at the woman, heart pounding, feeling everything. The emotional assault begins in my chest and rips through my body like a cleaver, hacking me to bits. I stand, too stunned to move, too shocked to flick the lighter. I had no hope, and never imagined she could be alive. My mind is arguing with me, telling me that this cannot be my mother, but my heart protests—and to my surprise is not dead. My heart's very much alive and trying to fill with hope.

I can't allow that.

I can't fathom this.

I can't light this.

But I can't let Vic live.

I can't do anything until I'm certain.

I can't. I can't. I can't. Those two words repeat in my mind as I stare blankly, feeling the slick plastic casing in my palm. There are a million reasons why I'm stuck in this loop. I cried at her grave. I wore her cross. I stole her ledgers. And, I paid for her sins. I missed her. I mourned her. I grieved her.

She's gone.

That's when Vic's voice purrs behind me, his breath washing across my cheek. "I brought you a gift, little sister. She's not in pristine condition, far from it." He sneers and then laughs lightly. "Sorry about that. I meant to shine her up, but you managed to evade my plans for this evening, so I thought it was time to show you exactly what you'll forfeit if you fail to comply."

I speak in a controlled snarl, still staring at the woman seated in front of me. "That's. Not. Her." My gaze locked on the figure in the chair and the familiar profile that's different but the same. I'm barely breathing, holding my breath, and remain frozen in place.

"Are you sure?" Vic's watching me with delight.

Mind fucks and head games. There's been so much hurt and anger seeping into my chest that I thought there was nothing left of me, nothing left to tear apart or rip away.

Maybe it's because he's dangling hope in front of my face that I'm reacting like this. There was nothing that could stop me, no one that could hold me back. Everyone I love is gone, dead. This is just another way to get me to back down. It's not Mom. It can't be. I steel my body and fist my hands at my sides, my thumb still on the lighter, ready to flick it.

"It's not possible." I've not turned away from the woman seated in the chair. The wind blows softly, lifting her tangled, filthy hair from her face. She doesn't say anything.

Vic strolls over to her, turning the chair around so I can see her head-on. The woman's eyes lock onto me, watching me as if she can't take me in, as if I'm not real. She doesn't speak. Her lips form a weary line, but those eyes are screaming.

Vic scuffs his feet against the gray stones of the balcony before offering a lazy grin my way. I don't move. I'm frozen, unable to take action. That's when Vic steps in close to me and presses his palms together. There's a look of triumph in his eyes, an intense need to gloat, and prove that he won no matter which hand I play.

He sniggers, glances at the woman and then back and me. He lifts a palm, inviting me to continue as he taunts, "Then finish your little attempt at arson. Blow up my home and everyone in it. Join me in the 9th Circle of Hell for all eternity."

"I didn't betray anyone I love." His words distract me for a moment, long enough to look away—long enough to think.

"Wrong on multiple accounts. You have so much to learn." He grabs hold of the woman's chair, and yanks it hard, sweeping it across the floor and into the powder room, stopping just before me. The centripetal force holds Mom in place. When the movement ends abruptly, she sways to the side but doesn't fall. Vic puts a hand on her shoulder to keep her upright. Mom's reaction is instantaneous. Her entire body tenses and pulls away from him, cowering. A tremor builds in the arm he touched and her jaw locks as she tries to keep from screaming out.

Vic chortles, steps toward me, and folds his hands together, clasping them in front of his narrow waist. Head lowered, he flicks his gaze back to the woman. "The lowest level of hell is reserved for the most despicable among us. The ones who betrayed their loved ones, the people they were supposed to protect. You and I won't even get the flames—we're not good enough for that. It's an eternity frozen in a sunless existence surrounded by people like me."

Think faster, Avery! This is bullshit. Light it already! "You're wrong."

He tips his head up, clears his voice, and looks me in the eye. "'As they denied all human ties, so are they bound only by the unyielding ice.'"

Anger surges through me. "Don't quote Dante to me to justify your actions."

He laughs, pressing his hands to his chest. "They're not my actions. Don't you see?" He gestures between us and bounces toward me with a massive grin on his face. "We're the same, you and I."

"No." The single word is clipped and certain. The muscles in my arms are twitching, ready to fight or run.

Vic leans in close to my face, still standing on the balls of his feet. His hands are held loosely behind his back, and he has a confident look on his face as if he's infallible. "We are alike, and you just don't want to admit it. Blood is thicker than water."

Rage boils inside of me, and I spew out, "WE ARE NOT THE SAME!"

His smile fades, and he tips his head to the side as he lowers himself to stand like he's not insane. He holds out a hand, palm up as if lecturing in a classroom in a calmly caustic tone. "Then prove it. Do it. Drop the lighter and forfeit your life to save hers."

I glimpse back at the woman in the chair. Her eyebrows pull together, and she's yet to say anything more than my name, but I feel it. My flesh covers in goosebumps and my heart is screaming with unrelenting vigor. I swallow hard and look down at the lighter in my palm.

I suck in a jagged breath and lift my chin. I tilt my head back toward the ceiling, trying to think, but I can't. All my thoughts are fractured, broken, and fall from the skies of my mind like tiny stones. One after another, they tumble into the abyss. It's only been a moment since I stepped foot in this room, but it feels like a lifetime.

The woman coos, her voice barely audible, "He can't stop you. Please, light it. You have my blessing."

There's a thud at the door as something huge barrels against it. A disgusting grin slithers across Vic's face. That door will fly open at any moment. The gas will dissipate, and my chance to end this battle will be lost. One flick of my thumb will repay this bastard for every wrong he's ever done. It will keep Vic from hurting anyone else. I'm justified. I can end this. The time to act is now.

But I can't move. That's the problem. My heart realizes the truth before my mind can process it. That voice, the inflections—I know it well. Even parched and weak, I know it's Mom. The words are falling away as I remember her vividly. Everything I lost and the pain of it comes crashing back all at once.

I have my mother back for a fraction of a second. It's goodbye again with no time for words, no apologies or explanations. Tears sting my eyes, and I question how it's even possible. I wonder if she shocked my soul back to life only for it to die a moment later.

Vic watches me carefully, the lines of his face creased in a gleeful grin. He stands there, daring me to light it—knowing that I won't.

I rub my thumb over the ridges on the lighter without sparking it while my other hand grips the pliers tighter before resting on my belly. My past and my future are at my mercy, but I don't know if it's more merciful to take their lives or spare them. I'm trapped, unable to decide, unable to move.

There's another slam at the door. When Vic's men break through, Mom will be gone again. They'll snatch her away. Vic will kill me—or worse. If he lets me live, he'll figure out a baby is growing within me. I can't fathom what he'd do to her, how he'd make her suffer. The time for action is now. If I wait, I'll lose my opportunity. I lift the lighter.

Mom nods at me and then meets my gaze. "Do it. You have our blessing."

I watch her lips wrap around the word, the way she says 'our' and the way her eyes lower to my belly—to the child yet to be born. It unhinges me. There's another crash at the door and a loud crack. The doorframe is splintering. One more hit and they'll be inside.

We're too high up to jump, and there's no other exit.

My only weapons are a lighter and a pair of pliers. Mom is too weak to walk. If I try to save her, I'll have to carry her. We'd never get away.

Mom's voice is louder this time, near frantic, "Avery, please!" She looks past me to the door that's splintering into pieces. Arms are shoving inside, but the wood is unyielding. Last chance. I lift the lighter, ready to strike. Willing to do it when a location check goes off.

In rapid succession, more male voices offer positions and check in with their location inside the building. They're responding, coming at Vic's silent request.

I lift the ridges of the lighter and take one last glance at the woman I thought I'd never see again. "Goodbye, Mom. I love you."

Her gray eyes flash with hope as a false smile falls from my lips. I put pressure on the metal wheel, turning it, gaining the force to flick it down and make the flint ignite.

Just before I finish flicking it, the last male voice buzzes in my earpiece.

"S17, secure." The deep timber, the way his tone is firm and unforgiving—I know that voice. I've heard it before, fierce and desperate.

It's Sean.

CHAPTER 14

Sean's in the house. He's alive. No, he can't be. I don't know if this is another manipulation or if it's real. I glance at my mother and then back towards the door. The wall shatters. Fragments of wood go flying through the air and burst into the main chamber of the room. Larger pieces travel with such force that they hit the wall and plunge into the plaster. Fragments of shiny black timber fall to the marble floor in a splintery rain. The room fills with large snarling men, their faces livid. Two grab me by the wrist and then secure their grip under my arm. The man to my left rips the lighter out of my hand while the rest of his squad opens the windows and examine the leaking gas fixture.

Vic strolls in behind them looking impish. His chest is puffed up, and there's an amused smile toying at his lips. He lightly places his hands behind his back as he approaches me. "And I thought we were going to have a family reunion in Hell today. Me, you, dad, and the bitch." He shrugs after tipping his head toward Mom.

The onslaught of incoherent rage is deadly. My field of vision fills with bursts of light that bleed red as I glare at my brother. I don't move, scream, or cry. No sound could communicate what I feel.

Vic is utterly calm. "Guess it wasn't meant to be. Or maybe you didn't have the balls after all, did you, little sis? Did Mommy here throw you off your game?" He's close, gloating in my face, preening like a deranged peacock. He grabs me by my neck, and squeezes hard, sneering in my face, "I win."

The fury within me explodes. It doesn't matter that he's choking me. I still manage to jerk my knee up, hard. The sudden displacement of my weight makes his thugs tighten their grip on the tops of my arms. I swing between the thugs like a toddler, connecting my knees in rapid succession with Vic's nuts.

Vic bellows as he folds in half, his hand swiftly flying and connecting with my cheek. The hit is hard enough to make tiny flashes of light twinkle like fireflies. It mingles with the red that was already there. Mom tries to move toward me, but as soon as she stands, she falls to the floor.

Gasping, I try to twist free. I thrash, kick, and then attempt to drop down, but they don't let go. Vic rights himself and gingerly places a hand on my shoulder before he buries his fist in my stomach. All the air gets knocked from my lungs, and I rasp, unable to breathe.

That's when he whispers, "You'll pay for that a hundred times over by the time I'm done with you."

I'm jerked to my feet. My brother grabs the hair at the base of my neck and pulls hard. I stumble forward. He snaps at his thugs, "Release her!"

They drop my arms and step back. Vic pulls my hair once more, forcing me to look up at him. His eyes narrow, and his lips twist with malice and lust. His mouth comes crashing down on mine as he paws at my breast and mashes our bodies together. My mother cries out from the floor, her hand outstretched toward me. The more I try to fight Vic off, the more he beats me down. His mouth crushes me, as his tongue slides into my mouth and his hand lifts my skirt, promising to terrorize me in ways I'll never forget.

I fight against him, but I'm unable to get away or peel him off. There's no leverage, no time. While shoving me to the stone wall, his tongue is in my mouth and his hand grips my ass. He pins me in place with one arm across my face while reaching for his zipper with the other. I do the only thing I can think of and bite down. Hard. The coppery taste of blood fills my mouth as Vic screams and jerks back. I can breathe, but the reprieve is short lived. I try to move away. Vic grabs me by the elbow, whirls me around, and tugs my hair, trapping me between his body and the wall. I go limp and drop to the floor and slither on the cold stone, almost crawling, as I try to get away from him.

Vic screeches, enraged, as he shifts his weight rapidly. Then his foot connects with my side. I'm hurled face-down on a pile of rubble. There's a sharp pain in my side when I try to breathe. My body is trying to curl into a ball. My fingers are on the pile of crap—fragments of stone and wood—as I attempt to push up. My head falls to the rubble, and a long shard of the wood presses my cheek, cutting my face. It's the size of a chisel and just as sharp. I try to lift myself off of it, but get slammed back down. Vic's hand presses against the center of my back, so I can't breathe. He holds me there like that, laughing. My lungs burn, and my arms flail as I'm prevented from inhaling. A sharp sting fills my chest as my face becomes hot and light. The corners of my vision go dark as blackness tries to overtake me.

That's when he removes his hand. "No way am I letting you pass out. You'll be awake and fully aware of everything I do to you. There's no escape. No way out, and best of all—you did this to yourself. You should have killed me when you had the chance, you stupid little fuck."

His greedy hands are at my hips, tearing the fabric away when the sound of cement rolling across the stone floor catches his ear. He pauses just long enough to turn and see a grenade with purple and green beads tied to the neck.

Vic freezes. We both stare at the sphere that looks like a bomb without a pin and wait for the explosion. Vic swats at the grenade that looks like it partied at Mardi Gras before the thing hisses. The same sound echoes all around me, filling the entire room with a shroud of smoke.

Sean's voice fills the air, but I can't see him. "Avery! Where are you?" He screams out, but the smoke is too thick.

The cloud of white obscures my vision and makes my eyes water. I blink rapidly, but it just makes it worse. It's like I Maced myself. My eyes burn and tear. Mucus fills my sinuses and drains out my nose.

I choke and try to get free, but Vic won't let go. He's still there with one hand on me, waiting for the smoke to disappear out the bay window. That's when the glass doors close, and three more grenades roll by us. I can hear them scrape across the floor as they come to a stop. The smoke thickens. Voices cry out around me, but I'm blind.

I knew I heard Sean, but I can't see him. I open my mouth to call his name, but Vic slams his hand over it. The bastard drags me further back into the room and away from the window. He hides in the slowly dissipating cloud. His men rush toward the smoke bombs when more familiar voices fill the air.

"Holy mother of hell!" Mel's voice calls out in one of the lighter fog banks by the door. The sound of metal on metal rings out as she laughs.

"Let's take these motherfuckers out!" Henry wails, and then promptly asks someone, "Did I say that correctly? It feels crass." He shrieks in the smoke, a willowy man lost in the clouds.

Mel snaps, "You're such a pansy. Are you sure you're straight?"

Henry growls, "You'll have to find out later, love. I'm busy at the moment."

"Promises, promises," Mel mutters. Sounds sweep around me of bones cracking and the floor becomes slick with blood. As

Vic tries to move me, he slips on something and stops abruptly.

I've not heard Sean again, but that doesn't mean anything. He'll remain quiet and snake through the crowd. He'll save me. I lift my head, trying to get off the floor, but Vic slams me down. When my temple connects with the marble, my vision blurs.

Through the rolling cloud of smoke, I see a single outstretched, mutilated hand. Mom. She's on the floor, alive. I watch her slender fingers curl and claw at the ground. I look at the nails that are non-existent stumps, peeled away and covered in blood and scars. Someone breaks the glass window and the smoke escapes into the night air. White tendrils swirl through the space, revealing people standing, fighting, around the edges of the room. Mom is across from me, closer to the door, her eyes locked on mine.

Vic shoves my face down again, hard. My cheek scrapes against the wooden plank between me and the floor, cutting my face open further. There's a sharp sting and warmth.

Vic hisses by my cheek, his intention very clear. He'll rape me with everyone present to show them he can, to prove he won. They won't be able to stop him. The smoke hasn't cleared, it still lays thickly on the floor.

The bastard hisses in my ear, his tongue tracing my skin. He's at my back, pressing me down. "It won't be as much fun not seeing the fear in your eyes, but I'm willing to make sacrifices. The Ferro's need to know their place and I intend to make it entirely clear, using you as an example of what happens to people when they fuck with Vic Campone."

A gun fires and the sound pierces my eardrum, making it hard to tell what happened, who got shot. There are still noises, but it sounds like they're talking from the bottom of a well.

Vic is still above me, his hands crushing my back to the floor with the promise of pain and torture. I can move my arm just enough to slip my hand beneath my face and grab the piece of wood that's pressing against my skin. I feel for it, wrapping my fingers around it and hold it tight. It's not long enough. It barely sticks out from my palm, but it's all I have.

Vic tugs at me and pulls my face up, screaming, "No one fucks with me, cunt. I'll make you beg for death, and then, if you're a very good girl—I might give it to you. But not tonight. I like to play with my toys first. The best part about owning someone is breaking them."

The mist obscures and partially hides us. I can barely see Vic since my eyes are still going batshit crazy from the smoke bomb, so I know he can't see me in any detail. There's as much tears and snot dripping from Vic as there is from me. He's a blur of a body.

I hold tightly onto the shaft of wood. Vic threads his fingers through the hair at the back of my neck and slams my forehead against the stone floor before grabbing my shoulder to flip me over. As he rolls me, the cocky ass is unguarded. Vic doesn't expect me to fight. I've been so docile, resisting just enough that he knows I haven't passed out. This is my moment, and I take it. I swing my arm wide and hurl the weapon in my hand toward his body.

The blurred movement doesn't register—Vic can't see the stake in my hand. He doesn't block me. I don't know if it's because he can't see the arc of my arm, or if it's because he's too arrogant to think I'd do it. Either way, there's no mercy in me. My rage has boiled past the point of comprehension. Every bit of strength, every ounce of anger, and every emotion that's fractured and fucked up my life channels into that hand. I slam the makeshift stake into his side. Vic's body goes tense as he jerks back and howls.

Vic releases me and falls to his uninjured side. His hands reach for the weapon lodged in his abdomen, but it's not there. I didn't let go, so the stake is still in my hand. Warm blood coats my skin, making my fingers slick. I crawl toward him through the looming smoke, reaching across the cold, slippery floor, and wail the stake into him a second time, not knowing what part of his body that I hit. His shriek turns to gurgling, quickly followed by nothing.

CHAPTER 15

Silence washes over the room as the sound of fighting ceases. The cloud of smoke that clings to the ground is dissipating. It doesn't hide everyone the way it had when Sean and Henry first chucked the nasty little orbs into the room. Long coils of white clouds blow out the balcony doors, escaping into the night. Suddenly, I can see what everyone is doing. As I sweep my gaze across the wreckage, I search for Sean.

Between the fog-like banks of clearing smoke, Mel stands over a prone man. There's a silver knife in her hand. She's breathing hard, waiting for him to rise, but he doesn't. Blood covers her hands and her hair is wet with it. Taut tendons lace her muscles so tightly she could crack.

Behind her, closer to the half wall that once blocked the door is Henry Thomas. He's wearing a once-white shirt, on the floor with another man, in a pool of blood. At first glance, it appears to be his. Henry is nearly prone on the man's chest, his elbows locked, with his forearm pressing hard on the thug's windpipe. There's a savage look on the Englishman's face. Henry's gaze catches sight of his shirt sleeves momentarily, making him sneer. It appears that Henry is more appalled at the state of his dress than the violence surrounding him. Bodies are littering the floor, twisted in ways that shouldn't be possible, caught in silent screams.

Pushing off the floor with one hand, I stagger to my feet and turn my head the other way. My dress is hanging off my body. It's held in place, lopsided on my body, still clinging by one shoulder strap. The front of the mutilated fabric is wet and warm. I gingerly press my fingers to the dress. Blood comes off on the pads of my fingers. I'm not sure if it's mine.

Dazed, I blink slowly and look for him— for Sean. He's standing over my mother, sweeping her off the floor as he lifts her in his arms. Vic's men lay in the wake of blood between Sean and the hole in the wall that once contained those massive black doors.

Everyone is frozen in a pose that reflects whatever they were doing when Vic's scream fell silent. The remaining men turn slowly to see their boss lying in a pool of blood on the floor at my feet. Their eyes lift to me slowly, shocked. No one speaks. Instead, they turn and flee, rushing through the smashed wall and out of sight.

Sean stands prone and lifts his dark head. When those blue eyes meet mine, I nearly lose it. There are no words that could possibly encompass the way I feel. Emotions rush through me making me feel like I'm metal in the microwave.

Sean's lips part as he watches me. There's something in his eyes, an emotion that's rich and pure. Words won't come, and I'm stuck in place, unable to move, not able to accept that this is over. That we survived.

My voice warbles when I try to speak, "I saw you die."

Sean shakes his head before he sits my mother in the chair. He leans down and says something softly to her. Mom nods once before Sean turns to me.

Sean's intense gaze holds mine as he walks through the final traces of the lingering fog before stopping in front of me. He tips his head down and places his hands gently on either side of my face. He rubs my cheeks with his thumbs and coos softly, "It's all right. It's over."

"I thought you were dead. I didn't know what happened—" My throat is so tight that my voice cracks.

He holds me close, presses my head to his chest, and then pulls back a little to look me over and smears his thumb through the blood on my cheek and the makeshift bandage around my head. "I'm all right. It's all right."

"The gas—" I look at the fixtures on the wall, worried it's still on, not entirely sure why I can't smell it anymore. Or why we're not puking on the floor from being poisoned.

"It's off, Avery. I shut it off. I couldn't let you—" he chokes on the words as his eyes sweep over me again and again. Sean cups my face in his hands and stands there, brimming with too many emotions all at once.

My insides are doing the same dance I see in his eyes. Anger and fear swirl together and scream like a banshee inside my mind. I slam my palms into his chest and demand, "Where were you? The bodies in the pool. I thought that was you!" I want to scream at him, but I'm still shorting out. My emotions turn on a dime and tears form as my anger recedes.

"I'm sorry," Sean whispers as he holds me, touches my hair and pulls back to make sure I'm really there. "Plans changed at the last moment. If it weren't necessary, I wouldn't have done it. I needed to guarantee that I could get to you—that I could pull you out of here. There's only one other person who could ensure it."

There's a loud thud—the sound of wood on stone—as Constance clears her throat in the former doorway that's now mostly rubble. She doesn't step over the threshold. Instead, she glares at me. "You and I need to speak, immediately."

I stare up at Sean, shocked. "You set her free?"

He nods. "When Black climbed into the car with you, I knew things were going to go to hell. Marty got hold of me on my cell before I got here. He said we were fucked, and needed another way out. Justin and Geek Guy, as you called him, were shot. Marty led Vic to believe it was Henry and me to give us more time."

"Marty killed Justin?"

"He deviated from the plan," Sean's hands touch my shoulders gently as he looks me over, still explaining, "That meant his loyalty was questionable. Marty knew the stakes and did what he had to do. With things that fucked up, there was only one person who could help."

Constance glares at me. "How touching." Her voice is dripping with anger as she studies her filthy red suit. It's covered in dirt and soot. Her hair appears as if she put her head in a wind tunnel and is sticking straight out from her scalp.

Sean glances at his mother, then whispers to me, "I'm still not entirely certain what her motives are, but she was our strongest ally tonight. She knew this place inside out and had access codes that allowed me to overtake the guards doing the perimeter check. Henry was able to disable the rest of the security."

Henry stands slowly and puts all his weight on one foot, either weakened or exhausted. He grips his left arm with his right hand and speaks to the room. "I couldn't go into the security room directly. It wasn't perfect, which is why Melanie was such an asset this evening. I found her on the way in, and we took care of the rest of the cameras leading up to this room the old-fashioned way while your betrothed hunted that animal." Henry glances over at Vic's fallen body.

Sean nods, then continues, "I found Gabe, and he told me what you were doing. I gave his men the eye drops Henry created, so the smoke bombs didn't incapacitate him and his men."

"I didn't know you designed those smoke balls." Mel grins at Henry.

He nods bashfully. "Nothing major, just a round housing with some natural irritants. I developed the eye drops and nasal spray while configuring the detonation mechanism after a few misfires in the lab." Mel watches him, practically beaming with pride. Henry smiles and shakes his head. "I like to dabble. It was nothing." Henry eyes Mel, nearly blushing.

"Where's Black?" I ask, wondering if she's dead or alive.

Sean's jaw tightens in anger. "I don't know. She's not dead, but she soon will be."

I shake my head and hold onto his arm. "Don't. She's the reason I'm still alive. Sean, she was trying to protect you."

"She did a shitty job and nearly killed you. If it weren't for her, you wouldn't have been sucked into this."

I shake my head, filling him in on everything that transpired between Black and me this evening. Then, I finally add, "If it weren't for her, I would have died before you met me. If she ran, let her run."

"If that's what you want." He watches me carefully.

I don't need a moment to decipher Black's true colors. "I do, let her go."

Sean wraps his arms around me again and holds onto me gently, careful not to hurt me. He breathes in my ear, "Anything you want. God, Avery, I didn't think I'd reach you in time. I thought I'd lost you. I was convinced you'd light up this place."

"I was going to," I explain and then glance at Mom. "I got sucker-punched when Vic showed me what he'd been hiding." I bite my lips hard and suck in a long pull of air that races out in a jagged rush. "This is my Mom." I extend a hand, introducing them and then start sobbing.

Sean wraps his arms around me, holding me like he'll never let go, and then his tears start as well. They fall freely, welcome, and weary. People talk around us, and there's a murmur of voices, but I can't focus on anything but Sean. So much has happened that I feel completely insane. I was mentally prepared to end everything, lose my baby, my life—and then Mom was there, and Sean wasn't gone. I feel caught between hysterical laughter and retching from the tumble of nerves uncoiling within me.

I don't know how much time passes like that before I manage to whisper in his ear, "I need to tell you something."

I've put off telling him about the baby. I didn't know how he'd react and honestly, it scares me. What if he's not ready? So much has changed since we spoke about picket fences and children. What if he's changed his mind? The pain in his voice when he talked about finding Amanda and losing his child still clings to the inside of my mind. What if he doesn't want to go through it? Pregnancy is uncertain, and there's no guarantee of anything. I've been beaten thoroughly tonight—what if the baby isn't all right?

Sean kisses the top of my head. "We need to take care of something first. Is that all right?"

I meet those beautiful blue eyes, and smile carefully before I nod. I'd rather tell him when we are alone. Clearing the tightness from my chest, I lean into him and ask, "What is it?"

Head bowed, he grins at the floor. "You'll see."

CHAPTER 16

This feels surreal. All of it. I'm experiencing sensations again. It's as if someone jump started my heart again and restored my ability to feel. Excitement mingles with exhaustion, and the only thing I want right then is to curl into Sean's arms and press my body against his chest in a big warm bed. That has to wait, though.

Men I've not seen before rush past, dressed in black fatigues with thick vests covered in pockets housing weapons and bullets, communicating through earpieces. Gabe follows close behind and beams a huge smile at me. He stops in his tracks, takes my face in his hands and frowns briefly before laughing and throwing his arms around me. "I didn't think I'd see you again."

Crushed by the bear hug, I wince and pat his back. The thick man steps away, suddenly regaining his composure. He inclines his head at Sean who is trying not to laugh. Gabe has been fairly stoic the entire time I've known him. On rare exceptions, he shows emotion, but it's usually anger—not this—not joy.

"Things changed," I smirk at him.

"I heard. Your mother is alive."

I avoid his eyes, afraid that I'll start crying again and slide my palm over my arm, smoothing the goosebumps. "Yeah, I didn't see that coming."

"I'm sorry, but neither did we. The morgue records indicated both bodies were identified and claimed. I never suspected that your mother was alive and hidden somewhere." He glances at Mom and inclines his head in a bow of respect before saying to me, "Some people couldn't recover from something like this. Let me be explicitly clear.

You are not one of them. You're strong, a fighter, and you'll heal. You both will. I'm glad you stuck around, Avery."

"Me too." My voice is so taut that it's barely audible. I force a smile. "So, I guess this place will be crawling with cops shortly. Shouldn't we leave?"

Gabe glances at Sean, and it becomes clear that they aren't telling me something. "Something like that. I need to take care of a few things. I want to hear everything, if you want to say it. But first, if you'll excuse me." Gabe rushes down the hallway.

We start walking again, and I say to Sean, "So that was weird."

"What do you mean?" Sean avoids my gaze and focuses on the carpeted floor leading down the corridor.

"Something like that?" I mimic Gabe's thick old dude voice and grin. "Fine, I don't want to know. I'm just not looking forward to giving a statement about any of this."

Sean squeezes my hand. "Don't worry, Avery. One thing at a time."

I'm walking through Vic's hallway with no fear. He's gone, dead. It wasn't until I stopped crying and noticed his body that I saw what I did to him. That piece of wood was sharp enough to puncture his skin but too short to hit any organs. Mel told me how to fight with a knife, and I must have held the shard the same way. When I swung, Vic must have moved because the stake caught the edge of his neck, puncturing it. My sick bastard of a brother drowned in his blood.

As Mel tends to Mom, I walk hand in hand with Sean into a room with a couch and a small fireplace. It's lit, crackling happily as if this was any other regular night.

Constance is sitting in a wing chair, appearing weathered and worn out. Her body is thinner than it should be. Her sallow skin is paper thin and shows scars that weren't there the first time we met. She doesn't watch me. Instead, her attention is on a furry white mountain at her side—the bear. The animal lifts its head and considers me for a moment, sliding those freaky pink eyes over my battered body.

Constance commands, "Rest." The creature lowers his head and doesn't move.

Gaping, I point at the carnivore sitting by Sean's mother. "Vic's bear ate someone. Why is it here?"

Constance snorts. "Because he's mine." She sighs deeply, too tired to explain, but there's no way I'm letting that go.

"You owned him first? Why?" My mouth is hanging open, and I regard Constance like she's insane.

Constance sighs and waves her fingertips in a small circle as if this is normal. "Security reasons, and unlike his second owner, I didn't announce that I owned this beast. So when I learned Vic was shopping for an intimidating pet, I had my people sell him to Vic. Bears are loyal to their first owner."

Shock renders me silent. Constance explains that she had the bear first, trained it, sold it to Vic without him knowing and then used it to attack his men to get into the mansion. Damn, she's devious. This woman is always ten steps ahead of everyone else and planning for things years in advance. Who buys a bear?

Sean crouches beside me. "I need to find a doctor for you, your mother, and mine. I'll be right back." He turns his attention to his mother, glaring at her cold eyes. The two of them stare like they might start fighting, but then Sean says, "Thank you." The words are sincere, painful, and utterly heartfelt.

Constance nods slowly to her son, confessing, "It was always for you."

Confusion dances across Sean's face. He remains still, waiting for more of an explanation. His mother sighs deeply and presses her fingers to her forehead and avoids Sean's penetrating gaze. "I had an agreement with Vic's father—let's call it a trade agreement."

Sean's jaw locks as his fingers dig into the arm of my chair. I press my palm on top of his, and he stills. "You were trafficking drugs?"

"Only things that the affluent wanted and couldn't find in tasteful social circles. It was a mutually beneficial arrangement, Sean. It put dirty little secrets in our pockets and cash in Victor's. It gave us power and position. None of New York's elite knew how I found out. They'd been so careful. They only used the man their friend used for drugs—heroin, crack, and those other disgusting vices. Not one of them realized I was the one who offered the first recommendation. That rumor began with me."

"Don't gloat, Constance. You were working with my brother. Don't deny it." My voice is firm but not forceful. I say it like a fact. Sean squeezes my hand.

She nods. Silence passes for a few minutes, and there's only the ticking of the mantel clock as the bear nuzzles his maw into his massive arm and closes his pink eyes. Then Constance swallows hard and lifts her gaze toward her son. "When the alliance with Victor Senior ended abruptly, there was a power vacuum. I wasn't able to secure it. Being in that kind of position created too many questions. I let things play out, which turned into a massive mistake. One misstep cost me dearly. Victor's son took the helm of that empire and then everything went to hell. Vic Jr., your brother, tied a rope around my neck when he started moving different merchandise."

"They weren't merchandise." I protest. "He sold women, and you helped him."

"Not just women." Constance looks me in the face, and I finally see the horror in her eyes. "Men and children as well. Some for sex, some for other purposes. I didn't ask. I vied my time until I could sever our business relationship but it became apparent that time would never come. I tried to protect my sons, behaved very badly, and did anything to distance them from the family—from me. I could accept the consequences for what I'd done, but I didn't want you to pay for my mistakes, Sean. And not Peter, and certainly not Jon. Your father," she shrugs as if he didn't matter, "the man has been on my shit list for two decades. They would have cleaned up a mess for me."

I flinch at her coldness. "You don't mean that."

She glares at me. "You have no idea what it is to take on another man's sins and wear his shame as your own." She glances at her son. "I warned you to keep your distance from her. I tried to protect you."

"You should have told me," Sean hisses through clenched teeth.

She shakes her head, ever proud. "Absolutely not. They were my iniquities, and I was willing to pay for them. As it is, the bulk of it landed on me."

Sean snaps, his voice cuts through the room, piercing my ears, "THE BULK OF IT LANDED ON AVERY! You did this to her! She killed her brother because of you!" Sean is in his mother's face, snarling. I'm up and at his side, my hand on his arm.

"That was inevitable and would have occurred without me." Constance explains, coolly. "I did what I could. I know you can't see it from where you stand, but Sean—"

The tension in his body nearly cracks his jaw. "I don't want to hear it. You lie. You've always lied about everything. You put Avery in the middle of this. You're the one responsible."

Constance drops her gaze and replies softly, "I am. This entire nightmare was my fault. There's nothing I can say to prove to you my motives were pure. You'll see what you see."

Sean stops breathing. He doesn't respond.

I ask him, "Can I talk to your mother alone for a moment?"

Sean's eyes shift to the side, glancing down at me as if I'd asked for a monkey or something else equally insane. But he doesn't protest. "Of course." He peers at his mother, pointing a finger at her as he chides the woman. "And make sure you tell her what you said to me." He retreats without another word, leaving me standing in front of his mother, studying her sickly form.

After the door closes I pad over to the wing chair opposite Constance and lower myself carefully into the seat. Everything is sore and hurting. "What did Sean want you to tell me?"

"That I've accepted you into the fold." She stares at me as the firelight dances across her face. Her expression screams that this acceptance was coerced, rather than sincere. She flicks her hand into the air and smirks at me. "Welcome to the Ferro family."

I laugh bitterly and pace in front of the fire. I stop after a few steps and cross my arms over my chest. I finally say, "You know something. Something that you didn't tell Sean."

She snorts. "I know a lot of things."

I glare at her. "You don't know everything."

A smile snakes across her face as she regards me. "Fine, we can trade. One piece of information that I'm not privy to for one secret relevant to you."

I sneer at her. "You don't know anything about me."

"Yes, I do. Your brother didn't put you in his crosshairs because of repressed mommy issues or jealousy—although the sick bastard had both those in spades." Her refined mannerisms are reemerging in front of the glowing flames. "There was a particular reason why he hated you so fiercely, and I'm confident that you are unaware. So if you want to trade secrets, you better have something of equal significance to trade."

I glower at her and fold my arms over my dress, smearing the blood across my pale skin. "I have a secret that will affect the Ferro fortune in perpetuity."

She scoffs at me, laughing. "No, you don't. There's nothing that could possibly…" she trails off and her brows knit together. "Tell me."

"You first." I don't trust her and probably never will. We stare at each other in a standoff until she finally rolls her eyes and swats a hand at me.

"Fine, but I'm tired of seeing you in that disgusting dress. It's dripping blood all over the carpet."

Looking down, I study the rug before lifting my eyes back up at her. "Why should I care? The cops will show up soon and—"

Constance laughs like fairies broke free in her concrete soul and are tickling her ribs. She swats a hand at me. "Cops. That's funny, dear. The police aren't coming. Ferro's clean up their own messes. Well, except for Sean and I suspect there's a story behind that event." She's talking about Amanda and I realize there's another secret she doesn't know.

"Really? You're not sure of your son?"

"Did you see how many men he killed to save you? He's a murderer."

"I suspect we all are after tonight." I meet her head-on and look her square in the eye. I tell her point blank, "He did not kill his wife. He loved her, he still does. You owe me two secrets now because you didn't know that."

Constance frowns at me but doesn't contest the addition of the second secret. She also doesn't try to tell me that she already knew the answer. "The carpet."

I glimpse at the rug under at feet. "What about it?"

"You don't want to drip blood everywhere because this is yours."

CHAPTER 17

Constance makes no sense. Why would I want Vic's rug? The confusion must be apparent, because she adds, "And you don't want the police here because you'll end up spending the rest of your life in jail."

I blink at her, still not getting what she's trying to insinuate. "Too late on that front—Gabe's already here. Dude is with the FBI."

"He is not working for the police," Constance explains with exasperation coursing through her tired body. She doesn't roll her eyes or snap at me. There are no visible signs of contempt, other than the unamused death-stare she's shooting my way at the moment.

I shake my head. "I'm too tired and have no clue what you're getting at, Connie, so spell it out."

She bristles at the informality with which she's addressed but doesn't comment on it. "Gabe was working in a different capacity tonight. That man hasn't worked for the FBI for a long time. He was on my payroll along with the rest of his new team. Surely, you've noticed how many unfamiliar faces are present this evening?"

No, not really. I had other things on my mind than playing spot the new guy, so I don't respond to any of that. Instead, I bounce back to her other statement. "What do you mean this carpet is mine? Are we rolling bodies out in it later?" I'm too tired to decipher her subtleties right now and wish she'd just tell me.

Constance snorts in derision. "No, little girl. This isn't that simple. Don't ask what happened to the bodies. You don't want to know. The carpet, though, that's a story you'll want to hear." She stares at the creamy rug and the sprawling pattern of blues and grays.

"So tell me. Why should I care?" I'm waiting for her to say something ridiculous or berate me, but her mood tempers and her voice sounds wearier than anything else.

"It's the reason why your brother took a nose-dive off the sanity bridge and pressed Black to the breaking point to secure you. He wanted to see you suffer. When the executor of his father's will explained things to your brother, he didn't take it well."

My brow lifts as my lips part. I finally shake my head and say, "What are you talking about?"

She snaps, waving a filthy hand in the air. "You're too obtuse. Your father knew about you and your mother—your birth father. Victor. He spent two decades trying to track you down. I knew you had a tie to the Campone family, but I didn't know what it was, so I had an eye on you too. His entire estate was left to the sole child of his first wife. That's you, my dear."

I stand without realizing it. "What? That's not possible. Mom and Victor weren't married. She wasn't his wife." I spit out the last word as if it's a curse.

"They were," she replies plainly, as she examines her filthy nails. "What you were told was a lie. I suspect your mother didn't realize that she got into bed with someone as evil as that man. Victor Senior had a way of sweeping a woman off her feet. He was charming when he wanted to be. When your mother figured it out, she took you and ran, then shacked up with your father."

"That's not true." I hiss again and stand up before realizing there's no place to go. I regard the bear, not wanting to go near it.

"Please, do you seriously think I'd make this up? Sit down." She points a tapered finger at my chair. "The truth hurts. Are you certain you want to hear the rest?"

I nod once and press my tongue between my teeth as I retake my seat.

Constance lets out a long sigh. "The will decrees that everything is passed to Victor's first wife, who was no longer living thanks to his idiot son. The wreck wasn't caused by your father—Vic Jr. arranged and carried out that plan. Your father was trying to find you. His son was already jealous of your mother. Victor didn't realize the plan his son set into motion until it was too late. By killing your parents, Vic Jr. thought he erased the competition. Apparently, he stashed your mother away. I had no idea. I thought they both perished."

"So did I," I say faintly.

There's a moment of silence before she continues. "Victor finally married Vic Jr.'s mother, but that freakish young man knew that if you appeared, he'd lose it all. He probably could have held onto everything, but not without bloodshed. Victor named you in his will. Nothing was left to his son or his second wife."

I blanch. "What do you mean? What's in Victor Campone's will?"

"It's written there in black and white— Avery Grace Campone is the sole heir of every possession, every business venture, everything."

"That's not my name."

"Yes, I'm afraid it is the legal name with which you were born. Avery Stanz doesn't exist. It's how your mother kept you hidden for so long. Have you ever seen your birth certificate?"

I make the same excuse my Mom made so many times, and it had seemed reasonable back then. "It was lost when we moved. I have one. I could have gotten another one, but the hospital where I was born burned down. Since it was before records were digital, there's no copy."

Constance smiles faintly, as if amused.

I add, "But the hospital burned, that part is true. I looked it up."

She sighs and shakes her head sadly at me. "Be that as it may, I can guarantee you weren't born there because the hospital where you were delivered is still standing in the center of Long Island, entirely unscathed—Good Samaritan Hospital."

"That can't be..." Shock fills me, and I don't know what to believe. After a moment of silence, I extend a palm toward her, urging, "Please continue."

Even if the story isn't true, I want to hear the rest. Maybe parts of it will make sense. Maybe there are kernels of truth lodged in with the lies. I don't know if I'll be able to tell them apart. And what do I say to my mother after all of this? I can't be angry at her for any of it. She lived in fear for so long. I just want her to feel secure and try to be happy and play with her granddaughter.

"Your brother was livid." Constance's expression goes dark. "He watched his father never give up on you, and the nail in the lunacy coffin came with the reading of the will. People say your brother's eye was twitching for days and he'd laugh when anyone tried to talk to him about it. After that, everything was downhill. He tightened his leashes on every business he had his fingers in and squeezed until you popped up. And lucky me, you were attached to my son."

"Sean found me."

Her icy eyes bore into mine. "I'd done everything I could concoct to keep Sean away, and you lured him in and held him here. He was never supposed to remain in New York." There's a fight brewing beneath the surface, but then she douses it. "It was my fault. He saw your file and knew I was interested in you."

"You had a file on me? What for?"

Constance sighs deeply and presses her fingers to her forehead. "Because Victor was searching for you. I thought you were an asset to be played. I didn't know you were his daughter until later. I was misinformed of your significance. The short version is that all of this is yours." She extends her arms, palms up, gesturing to the room.

The words fall upon me like a tidal wave. I don't understand. "Say what, now?"

"Everything." Constance arches a brow at me while placing her palms on the arms of her chair. "Your brother buried the lawyer who delivered the news, but the court already had the will. This is yours. Every asset is yours. Every mob affiliation is also yours, although I assume you'll pour glitter on it. I'd suggest you sell it off if you don't want it. Letting it sit is not a good plan."

I blink, shocked. All of this belongs to me? That can't be. "Can't another relative contest the will?"

Constance shrugs, which is odd for her. "I suppose your mother could challenge it, but I doubt she would. She tried to hide you from that man for twenty years. It would require admitting she was still married when my nephew shot her first husband."

I nod slowly and study at the dancing flames within the hearth. I don't want it, all this. It's blood money. Curiosity makes me ask, "How much is there?"

She laughs. "About as much as I have. Let's leave it at that." She steeples her fingers and meets my gaze. "Now, a secret for a secret. What do you know about my fortune?"

It takes me a moment to shift gears. I turn toward her and glance into her face. "There's a new Ferro to add to the succession for the estate." I force a smile, not sure how she'll react and place my hand on my belly.

Her stony countenance lightens for a moment as her fingers touch her lips and a giggle escapes. "A baby?"

"Yes."

"Does Sean know?" She appears truly delighted. I expected her to challenge the baby's legitimacy, to claim it belonged to another man. But she doesn't do that at all. Doesn't even hint at it.

I shake my head. "I've not been able to tell him yet. I didn't know if he'd want her. I mean, with everything that happened…" I trail off, leaving the painful memories out in the open.

Constance rises and steps toward me in two long strides. She wraps her arms around me and says into my ear, "He's ready." When she pulls back, she adds, "Tell him. It's time to lay old wounds to rest. It's time to put this chapter in the past. I've not seen him so fiercely devoted to anyone. Ever. I would have thought he'd hold his heart back after all that ugliness, but somehow Sean persevered and I know the exact reason."

"What is it?"

"It's you, Avery. You brought that man back to life and vanquished the monster he was becoming."

I glimpse at the carpet. "He was always a good man underneath." I glance up at her. "I wanted to be like him, and bury myself in that darkness. I never wanted to feel anything ever again. Instead of learning how he did it—"

Constance sniggers. "Your glitter rubbed off on him, and now he's all rainbows and sunshine, which appears to be contagious."

I snort a laugh. "Yeah, something like that."

"A word of warning," Constance asks me if it's alright and I can tell she's sincere. I nod in assent, and she continues. "Sean still thinks his life is made of eggshells that will swiftly crack if he makes a wrong move. Strong women don't like to be handled gently."

She levels her eyes to mine. It's the nicest thing she's ever said to me, and I don't doubt her genuineness. Something passes between us, a mutual understanding that we both will do anything necessary to protect our families, which will soon be one and the same.

Constance lifts a brow and smirks. "Knock him on his ass because this little event here tonight scared the shit out of him. He'll want to play it safe. Don't let him. You brought him back from the deep. Now you have to hold him here."

CHAPTER 18

The rest of the night passes in an exhausted blur. Sean's brothers appear on the site. Peter rushes at Sean and throws his arms around him. Jon doesn't wait his turn and slams into the two of them.

When they break apart, Jon promptly scolds his oldest brother, slapping Sean in the back of the head which makes hair fly into Sean's eyes. "You should have said something! I would have been here."

Peter gives more of the same, another swat the back of Sean's head with an exasperated expression on his face. "You should have said something! You scared the hell out of me. Mom called me. Mom. Do you know how weird that is? I thought you were dead."

Sean doesn't know what to do with the onslaught of affection. That crooked grin lights up his face as he punches them both in the arm in an affectionate sort of man-hello. Then he says to Peter, "You have a new wife." Sean inhales deeply and runs his hands through his hair, glancing between his brothers, confessing, "I didn't want to suck you two into this. I didn't want to pull you back into this shit. It's been messy."

Peter nods before he glances at me and walks over, leaving the other two talking softly and exchanging more man-punches. Peter's wearing a crisp white button-down and his face is covered in stubble. There are lines on one side of his cheek as if he'd been sleeping.

He goes to say something, smiles so brightly that it reaches his eyes, closes his mouth and then steps into me, wrapping me in a hug. His voice is in my ear, "If anything happened to you, Sean would be lost. Thank God, you're safe." He pulls back and rests his hands on my shoulders to look me over.

I'm covered in grime but too weary to care. I don't know what to say. I just stare up at him. Peter and Sean appear to be so similar but there's one major difference—there's light in Peter's eyes. Hope. I wonder if Sean will ever get there and be completely free to love and laugh again. It's as if Peter senses my thoughts because he says in a soft voice, "We all heal, Avery. Each at our own pace. Lean on him. You won't knock him down, and you never know—it might be exactly what he needs to finally be happy."

"Yeah?" I snort with an unconvinced smirk. "He needs a sad girl crying on him to make him happy?"

"Weirder things have happened." He wiggles his eyebrows at me. "Sometimes tears need to fall to make room for the sunlight."

"Always a poet," I smirk and watch Sean converse with Jon. Their conversation flows freely, and the apprehension, the wall that was between them is gone. Whatever sins that divided Sean and Jon were decimated tonight. I'm happy for them.

"You know it," Peter smirks at me. It's a smile nearly identical to Sean's, slightly crooked and completely charming. "Seriously, Avery. I'm glad you're safe."

Sean and Jon wander over together, and Sean asks, "Avery, can you give us a few minutes?"

I jest. "Family meeting with Mom?"

Sean glowers while Jon laughs, "An alliance with the winter witch."

I almost don't say it. I don't want them to think I'm naïve, but I'm too damn tired. "Your mother is a chess master—"

"No shit," Jon blurts out.

Peter shoves Jon's shoulder once, hard, to shut him up. And then Peter extends a palm toward me. "Please continue."

I glance between them, the three of the Ferro brothers standing side by side. I don't think they know, so I tell them. "You've suspected that you were the pawns and your mother was the queen. But you three were never pieces she was willing to lose. She was the queen—still is—but you guys are the one bit that ends the game for her. You're the king. All three of you were always that piece to your mother. She'll protect you at all cost and not stop until she's won."

Sean is taken aback a dark brow lowering above a sapphire eye. The corner of his lips quirks up, surprised. "You're defending her?"

"No," I say plainly and look up at the man I love. "I'm telling you what I see. You were never expendable. She just made you think you were. If I could have saved my mom from everything she's suffered, I would have done the same thing." There are tears in my eyes when I say it. "Sean, the two of you have been playing for the same team this entire time."

"Why are you so certain?" he asks and I can't blame him. It's been horrific to watch Constance's plans play out only to end up with another knife in your back. With Constance, there is always a reason.

"Because," I confess with complete certainty. "I'm no longer on the chessboard. Distance makes it incredibly clear. So does hindsight. She tried to move all three of you out of check and the only way to accomplish that was to force you out. You guys were pretty much estranged when I met you. Now you're not. Your mother is a frightening woman, but she had your back through all of this. I'm certain of it."

Sean steps toward me and takes my hands in his. "I believe you."

I smile carefully, feeling way too vulnerable. "You don't think I'm foolish?"

He laughs, and it's a deep rich sound. "Of course not. You have more perspective on this than I do. Can we trust her?"

I meet three set of blue eyes, one at a time, and then nod slowly. "I think so, but trust should be earned. Offering to start over is more than she imagines. She doesn't expect your forgiveness. You can let things fall as they may, but if you want to be a family again, I could see it happening."

Three crooked smiles on three men, each standing on his left foot with the right knee slightly bent, and sculpted arms folded across a broad chest. They nod once, tightly, in unison letting me know they've heard what I had to say. Peter's hair falls into his eyes. When he pushes it back, he turns, followed by Jon. The two men walk shoulder to shoulder down the hall, away from us.

Sean steps closer to me, kisses my grimy cheek. "You're incredible. What did you want to tell me before?"

"We'll talk later." I wave a hand at him, gesturing for him that it's all right to leave. "Go confer with the Queen."

Sean smirks. "She won't like that nickname."

"It's better than the previous one." I grin wickedly.

Sean snorts and hugs me once more before hurrying to catch up with his brothers. They walk together ready to face whatever's next. If that powerhouse learns to work together, they'll be able to do anything.

CHAPTER 19

I'm drooling on myself and half-conscious by the time the doctor finishes with my mother. I'm still in Vic's house, in a room down the hall from the Ferro clan meeting. My mom is lying on a couch with her hands folded together on her chest. She remains perfectly still, in a coffin-esque pose. The older man is wearing scrubs as if he were pulled from surgery at the local hospital. Good Sam, as the locals call it.

He's a narrow man with sunken eyes, white hair, and a large hook-shaped nose. His features are sharp and unforgiving. He's all angles and muscle, even under-aged skin with a sprinkling of sunspots on his forearms. He's wearing blue scrubs with a white t-shirt. It pokes out from the V-neck top. He crosses the vast room where I'm sitting on the edge of an armchair.

He towers over me, and I rise. He extends his hand and speaks in a deep voice, like James Earl Jones' baritone territory. "Miss Stanz? How are you feeling?"

We shake hands briefly. "I've been better, but not bad, considering everything. How's my mom? What happened to her?" Then a bit of panic strangles me and I blurt out, "It is her, right?" I need someone to confirm this. I'm so afraid to accept it and the shit-ton of emotional crap that will come flooding in when I do.

The man bows his head and slightly wrinkles his brow as he peers over his shoulder at her. Mom hasn't moved. Her chest rises and falls slowly with her gaze locked on the ceiling. When the doc lifts his head, he explains, "I can confirm that this is your mother. I'm afraid most of her fingerprints were removed. However, I was able to ascertain her true identity using her dental records. It's her."

"Thank you." I'm watching my mother and a moment of silence passes. It's really her. We get another chance.

"She went through a lot, Avery," the man offers solemnly.

I'm almost too afraid to ask. "What did they do to her?"

He asks me flatly, "Do you really want to know? Your brother was cruel and tortured her relentlessly. I'm shocked she's still alive, to tell you the truth. Her body tells a graphic story of all she endured. Not speaking very much at this point is expected. Still, I can put the pieces together. I know what they did to her."

I swallow hard and tighten my arms across my middle and hang my head, shaking it. "Maybe I'm a coward, but I don't think I can bear it right now."

He places a hand on my shoulder. "There's not a drop of cowardice in you."

I laugh bitterly and try to step away, but he doesn't release me. "I doubt that."

He tips his head to the side and meets my gaze. "Fear debilitates most people and keeps them from taking action. You did what you had to despite being afraid. You saved your friends and your mother."

"I killed him." I blurt it out and swallow a sob swiftly. My face crumbles as my mouth twists as I try not to fall apart. Tears flow down my cheeks in twin rivers. I hate crying, but I'm so weary that I can't hold it back any longer.

I swat at my face, wiping the dampness away. "Why am I crying? Vic was a horrible person. I feel like I can't breathe." I clutch my neck and inhale sharply, trying to eradicate the invading emotion. I don't want to mourn him. The residue of existence stained me forever, and I'm blubbering about it.

"If you weren't crying," the doc says, "you would be a horrible person. Avery, you'll grieve his loss like he was family because he was family." I feel his kind eyes on me, waiting for me to look up, but I can't.

"No, he wasn't," I retort sharply, still wiping my eyes and cursing under my breath. "He may have been blood, but he wasn't family."

"Your heart doesn't know the difference."

I gawk up at him. "That's not fair. Are you serious? This is actual grief? I'm not crying for me?" It feels selfish, like I'm a tearful asshole because I've killed someone. Again. I can't even think about it. It's like my brain is trying to shove a chicken back into an egg. It doesn't want to go there.

"Of course you're crying for you." The doc walks over and sits beside me. He glances across the room before smoothing his palms over his scrubs.

"How could you possibly know that?"

The man doesn't search for the right words. They just tumble out. "Because I know your story. Avery, you lost so much. You thought you were alone, found out you weren't—had family—and then discovered your brother was the one who ruined your life and killed everyone you loved. You should cry for you, for things going the way they did. Bottling up emotions won't help you. Venting, crying, and dealing with what happened will help you get past this. You won't forget, no one would expect you to, but you can move forward."

"Who are you?" I meet his eyes, slightly unnerved that he knows so much about me although I've never met him. "I thought you were a doctor on call for the Ferro family. That's not the truth, is it?"

His gaze flicks to the floor as he takes a breath and pauses. When he glances at me side-long, he adds, "It a partial truth. I am a doctor for the Ferros. I met Constance when I was working an ER in Aruba. She offered me a job here anytime I wanted it. At first, I declined." He clears his throat and avoids my eyes, studies his hands. "I remember you."

The words are less confident than the others. Almost as if the doc wasn't sure he should have said them. "What do you mean? Remember me from what?" I sniffle and try to keep my nose from running down my face.

The doc plucks a clean handkerchief from his pocket and extends his hand toward me. "I was there when you were delivered. Then I helped you and your mother escape."

I take the hankie and dab my eyes and glance over at him, surprised. "You were?"

"Yes," he says. "It was an unusual situation. It was a delivery in a hospital back when we didn't ask if the mother or child was in danger. I was young and idealistic, barely into my first year. No one looked twice at me when I wheeled you two outside and put you into a cab."

I regard the man who protected my mother. "Did you know her back then? Mom, I mean."

He nods his head. "Yes." The word is barely a whisper. He avoids my gaze for a moment and explains, "I knew her when she was young. There are some people that you never forget, and she was one of them." He smiles but it's bittersweet, as if there'd been possibilities with Mom at one point, but then they turned to dust.

"You loved her?" It's beyond blunt, but I see it in his eyes. Once upon a time, this man cared very deeply for my mom.

He nods once, and it's barely perceptible. "She was a good friend, back in high school." He doesn't comment further on their relationship. Instead, he continues telling my story. "She insisted that you be kept with her at all times and even followed you down to the nursery. New mothers can certainly be protective, but not to that extreme. I knew something was wrong because I knew her. She wouldn't let you out of her sight. It made me wonder, and I finally asked if something was wrong. The expression on her face said everything."

"She told you about Victor?"

He shakes his head. "She didn't have to—I knew something was very wrong. She was so afraid. I did something drastic, and acted because she was a friend. There are certain people you can't walk away from, certain people you take risks for, no matter the cost. I hoped I did the right thing by granting her wishes and sneaking the two of your out of the hospital. I took your lives into my hands and often wondered what happened to you both—if it was mercy or a mistake. I'd hoped that if I couldn't find you, neither could Victor."

Mom never spoke about this man, and I can't help but wonder why. I suppose it would be odd to talk about an old friend once she married Daddy. I file the facts away so that I can talk to her about it someday.

Then I confess, "It was mercy. Mom had a few moments of joy between the shadows. I remember her smile, the times she forgot to look over her shoulder and got lost in the moment."

The doc is quiet and then glances to the room across the hall. "You should talk to her."

Reluctance slithers around my neck, and I confess, "I don't know what to say. I feel so guilty like this was all my fault. Even if it wasn't, it all happened because of me." I'm wringing my hands and getting dangerously close to hitting the exhaustion wall. There are things I want to say to her, questions to ask. Anger and joy mingle in my chest along with remorse and relief. It makes me mute.

He nods slowly, making sounds of understanding, then lifts a palm, asking, "What if she feels the same way?"

I reply softly, "She shouldn't."

"Neither should you, but you do." He presses his wrinkled lips together and changes the subject. "Can I look you over? I know you're hurting."

"Yeah," I murmur. I sit down on the edge of the coffee table and stare at an ugly painting on the wall and the thick golden frame.

The doc examines me, treats the wound on my temple, cleaning it and applying liquid stitches. The doc talks as he works, telling me about what he's done since he last saw me, how he left the States and worked at a medical mission in Uganda before moving to Aruba a decade ago. He didn't come home until recently when he heard that Victor Campone died. He always thought they'd find him. When he saw the headline that Campone was shot, he called Constance and asked if that job was still available. He's been on staff ever since.

He dabs ointment on my cheek, "In the meantime, I did what I could, where I could. It's not much, but one life touches another and so on." His voice is soothing and keeps my mind from bouncing haphazardly.

"My mother used to say that."

He chuckles softly and glances at her. "Is that so?"

I nod. "Yeah, I suppose that's where I got it from, and it's why I couldn't give up on Sean, despite all the things people said about him. He changed. Vic didn't."

"Or maybe neither of those men changed at all. You saw Sean for what he is beneath all the turmoil. You also saw Vic for what he was as well. Having faith in people can bring out the best in them, but I don't believe we ever truly change. We just continue, moving forward, with scars that remind us of our mistakes. A man who can look in the mirror and remember those errors is far less likely to make them in the future."

I shake my head and smile up at him. "You're a walking oxymoron. You know that? You think you can't save anyone, but you spent twenty years literally saving people. I think there's a disconnect between your head and your heart." Like calls to like and in this case, I know he's like me—wanting to see the best in people and always hoping. It's a precarious way to live, but that's the point. He lives. He doesn't shrink back and withdraw from the world.

The doc offers a grin and places his hands on his hips and laughs lightly. "Touché. The world needs more people like you. Straight and to the point. So, Avery, is there anything else I should check before I tend to the others?"

The smile falls from my lips as I ask, "Is the baby alright? I just found out that I'm pregnant and I'm almost too afraid to ask. Vic hit really close." I touch my side gingerly and wince. I'm sure there's a flowering bruise creeping up my ribs.

"I can check. How far along are you?"

I tell him I'm not certain, but maybe eight weeks or so. He presses the stethoscope to my belly and is too quiet. He listens for a long time and then puts it down. When he looks at me, I'm so afraid.

"Is she all right?" My voice chokes. I can't swallow. "You can't hear her heartbeat, can you?"

"I shouldn't be able to hear anything yet, but I can. I suspect that you're further along than you guessed. Maybe ten to twelve weeks?"

"She's okay?" I cover my mouth with my hands as I try not to cry. I kept thinking I'd never see her. I figured I'd lost her.

"Yes, she appears to be fine. We can run more tests tomorrow just to make sure." He smiles broadly at me as I start to cry. I'm shaking and trying to stop, but I can't. The emotional firehose takes over and there's a spray of tears and worry in my soft sobs.

A slight touch is on my shoulder a few moments later. Mom is standing there, lips parted, looking down at me. Her expression caught between pride and joy.

"You're having a baby?" The corners of Mom's mouth twitch as her lips pull into a smile. "Oh, Avery. I thought that was why you put your hand there like that, but I didn't want to say anything. I wasn't certain until just now." She wraps her arms around me, and we both cry, sitting on top of a tiny table in front of the fire.

CHAPTER 20

I hadn't planned on talking to anyone
about the baby before I spoke with Sean, but
the way tonight played out didn't go that way.
When Sean finishes with their meeting, Peter
offers to take Mom to the Ferro home in the
city.

I stare at Sean, "Your family has an
apartment? Why the hell were you in a hotel?"

He lifts a brow at me with a crooked
smirk. "I was trying to keep you away from
them."

"That didn't work out." I snort a laugh and pad over to Sean, bone weary. "Please tuck me in."

"Of course. Where are we staying? I heard you've come into some money and you don't need me anymore," he says teasing before pressing a kiss to my forehead.

I lift my hand and press my finger to the tip of his nose. "Now you know, without a shadow of a doubt, that I did not choose to marry you for your money."

"I knew that before today." He watches me carefully, his eyes boring into mine.

I'm close to his face, leaning into his chest. His brothers are in the hallway, talking to each other. Jon laughs loudly, and Peter's face turns red. Peter is the shy version of Sean, while Jon is the adaptation that says everything he's thinking. The three of them are lucky to have each other.

"So, where should we sleep? I suppose that you would rather not stay here." Sean cocks his head to the side and glances down at me, dark lashes soft against his skin.

I frown and shake my head. "No, I never want to step foot in this place again. As soon as it's out of probate, this house is gone."

"Good." He's tender, sweet, and kisses my brow as he ignores his siblings who are waiting for him. "I also thought you'd like to be near your mother and arranged for it. We'll head over with her in a moment. I'm sure you two have a lot to talk about – I heard she's speaking. That's an excellent sign."

Yeah, a baby would make anyone talk. I'm afraid Sean is going to hear the news from someone else. Admiring his beautiful face, I whisper, "I need to tell you something."

Sean presses a kiss to my forehead. "So tell me." He peers down at me as if he's expecting me to blurt it out right here, right now.

"It's kind of private." I glance at his brothers who are still in earshot.

"Oh," he grimaces. "You can tell me when we get to the house."

—

The Ferro home in the city turns out to be a massive penthouse on Park Avenue. I don't know why I'm shocked, but I am. It's immaculate, decorated in a similar style to the Ferro mansion in deep colors, posh fabrics, and ornate decorations. I gape as we walk inside.

Constance will show up here at some point as well. With the Ferro mansion still in pieces, there's nowhere else to go. Sean assures me that we can find our own place quickly. Even with my inheritance tied up, he has plenty of money to get whatever we want—even a little cape cod with a white picket fence. If I could have any home, live anywhere in the world, I'd still pick that little house in the suburbs of Manhattan.

After scrubbing off all the gore and grime, it's nearly sunrise. The horizon grows brighter, chasing away the night. I stare out the window, lying on my side, in a warm bed waiting for Sean. My eyelids lower and then dart open a few times.

That's all I remember until I wake up with Sean's warm body next to mine a few hours later. He's breathing deeply, slowly. His dark lashes are like black fronds against his smooth cheek. I close my eyes and fall back to sleep.

When I finally rouse, I stare off the edge of the bed. There's a thin slit of orange sunlight on the hand-carved wood floor. I stare at it sleepily and wonder if it's dusk or dawn. I don't even know what day it is and I really don't care. I roll over and find Sean awake with his eyes on me. His hair is tousled and dark stubble lines his jaw.

He smiles at me and gently strokes my hair. "Hello, Miss Smith. How are you this evening?"

I grin at him and stretch carefully. Every muscle aches and my head is throbbing. "I feel like I had the shit kicked out of me last night. Oh wait, I did." I scoot closer to him and rest my head against his chest. "When did life get so weird?"

"The moment I met you." He grins down at me before squeezing me lightly, being careful to avoid the sore spots.

"Hey!" I tip my head back to look into his face which bears a pleasant expression. His lips curve up as if he has a secret. "There's something different about you today. Or tonight. Whatever it is."

"Oh?" He grins broadly and then laughs, delighted. Then he leans in close and whispers, "I know your secret."

I frown unable to conceal my disappointment. "Someone told you." Indignant, I sit up and jut out my lip. "Who would do that?"

"My mother. Who else?" He's laughing, completely happy.

"Sean," I whimper softly, "I wanted to tell you."

"I know, but I was awake for a little bit earlier, and it came up."

I hesitate for a moment. "You're happy about it? I didn't know how you'd react if you were ready or not."

"Of course I'm ready."

I smile, relieved. "Thank God. I didn't know what you'd do. I mean, it's a big deal—"

"Avery, you're spectacular. You know that right? You are completely perfect," he preens, bursting with pride. There's still a big playful smile on that gorgeous face.

"So you're okay with it?" I'm still cautious, and shocked he's so pleased. I thought he'd be anxious about a baby, about settling into a life together.

"I'm fucking elated." His hands are flying as he talks, animated and cheerful. "Seriously, no one has ever done what you did and lived to tell the tale."

I blink at him. Silence. He's still laughing and stops when I don't say anything. After a moment, I lift my finger and confess, "I don't think we're talking about the same thing. 'Live to tell the tale' isn't exactly flattering for you. I guess it's accurate...sorta." I snort a laugh and try not to smile.

Sean arches a brow at me. "Why, what are you talking about?"

"No," I shake my head. "You tell me what you're talking about first."

He eyes me suspiciously. "Mother told me what you talked about last night. About you standing up to her. She said that you didn't back down and traded secrets like a pro. She told me this morning that I found a good one, and not to fuck it up." He laughs for a moment, then adds, "What were you talking about?"

I start laughing and do a faceplant onto the bed and instantly wish I hadn't. I'm so sore. I chuckle into the sheets, instantly happier. He doesn't know about the baby. I get to tell him. Elation and anxiety mingle together and bounce through my muffled laughter.

Sean lays across my back gently, careful not to crush me, and pulls my shoulder up in an attempt to see my face. "Avery, what's so funny?"

"Besides the fact that your mom likes me?"

"Yes, although that's a reason to smile." He nuzzles a kiss against my neck and repeats, "Tell me your secrets, Miss Smith." The warmth of his breath wisps over my ear as the scent of him fills my head.

I swallow hard, heart pounding, and glance over my shoulder at him. Those blue eyes are curious and lingering so close, with lips near enough to kiss. "Well, I have a secret."

"I know you do." The corners of his mouth tip up into a sexy grin.

"I'm not sure I want to tell you yet," I tease, still smiling at him broadly. With a flick of my hand, I add, "I mean it's pretty major."

He tickles my neck with a seductive kiss. "All the more reason to share." Stubble lines his face along with a nasty gash and bruise that runs up his arm to his shoulder. "Miss Smith, Avery, My Love—tell me."

I press my lips together and then blurt out, "You're going to be a daddy." I catch my lower lip in my teeth as time stands still. The moment is surreal. Everything feels a million times louder, slower, and more colorful— more important.

His voice is soft, surprised, "Are you serious?" He pulls away to sit up. I roll over to watch him and the way his eyes seem to be filling with hope. "How do you know?"

"Yes, I'm serious. And I know because the doctor confirmed it." More tension makes things intensify. After a nervous giggle, I add, "And I peed on a stick. It's legit."

His eyes are searching mine, looking for something he can't find before they drop to my middle. When he glances up at me, he asks, "And it's all right? You were hurt. Is he…?"

"She's alright. I think it's a girl."

He smiles softly, in awe. "We're having a baby?" I nod, and nerves lick the insides of my stomach. "We're having a baby!" He shouts and grins at me, full wattage.

Sean leaps up and dances around the room, naked, forgetting himself for a moment. Contagious excitement bounces through the room as I sit on the bed and giggle. Sean dances like a leprechaun, kicking up his heels and swinging around the bedpost. All he needs is a green top hat.

Then he bounds onto the bed, pulling me closer to him and then takes my face in his palms. "Why didn't you tell me sooner?"

"I tried. Stuff kept happening—"

His mouth is on mine, kissing me hard, smiling while he does it. "I love you. I am so crazy, fucking in love with you. You have no idea. None. I feel like my heart is going to explode with glitter." He's up on his knees and laughing. He takes my hands and stands us up in the middle of the mattress. "Do you see what you do to me?"

"I didn't do this. You've always had the Lucky Charms guy living inside you. No wonder why you never talked to anyone. That seems a little bit cray cray, Sean."

"Only good things come in green tights." He barks a loud belly laugh.

"I've never seen you act like this. Has there really been a repressed happy guy in there all this time?" I place my hand on his heart.

His voice is deep, filled with mirth that's warm and full. "I have no fucking clue, but it feels like I could do anything right now. Avery, my God…" He inhales sharply and jumps. When his feet hit the mattress, I fly upward. If the ceiling weren't nearly twenty feet tall, I'd hit my head. We're all giggles, holding hands, and laughing until there's a loud crack at the foot of the bed and the bed frame snaps, making us topple over.

Sean, blue eyes glittering, leans over me. "I'm sorry, are you okay?"

"Yes, but you broke the bed. Your mom's gonna kill you!" I tease before we deteriorate into laughter.

Then there's a knock at the door and a voice asking if we're all right.

Sean jumps up, grabs a robe, ties it, and throws open the door. Constance is standing there, bleary-eyed and hair a mess. "What on earth was that sound? The ceiling shook. Sean?" She meets her son's eyes at the same time he grabs her shoulders, forgetting himself, and pulls her into a bear hug.

Sean releases his stunned mother a moment later. "I'm going to be a father and the baby is going to call you Grammy." He waggles his eyebrows at her and then bounds down the hallway hollering, "I gotta tell Pete!"

I'm still sitting on the broken bed smiling after him, wearing one of Sean's t-shirts. Constance glances at me. "I told you he was ready." She hides a knowing smile before arching her eyebrow and looking at the bed. Then says, "I don't want to know what you two were doing in here."

"It's not like that. Hey!" She's gone, closing the door before I can explain.

Sean whoops from the end of the hall, his voice echoing back toward me. I've never seen him so happy, never heard that much inflection in his voice, ever. It's as if his bindings finally broke free. If there was one thing holding Sean down, it was Sean Ferro. Joy eradicates fear, fries it up until there's not a drop left. I saw the emotions splayed on his face, fighting for control. Today joy won and fear lost.

Today will be different, and I can't stop smiling about it.

CHAPTER 21

The strangest things happen when you least expect them. I worried about Constance ripping my mother's frail emotional state to shreds. I mean, the woman was barely talking. Mom retreated so far into herself to survive the terrors that met her daily for months on end. There was no break, no time to gather herself and rebuild her mental state during that period. The doctor warned me that she'd need a lot of patience and understanding. Trauma victims tend to behave differently, and the slightest thing could set her off and cause her to regress—a turn of phrase, a sight, or smell.

I walk on eggshells around her, but not Constance. At first, I berated Constance for it, but she didn't listen to me. She explained, "Acting as if she's broken will only keep her that way."

Constance is a paradox of a person. She's fierce and kind with my mother. I don't understand how she's both at once, but it doesn't send Mom back to the darkness. I watch the two of them together and know they've shared more time talking than they let on. They seem to have more in common than a grandbaby and the misfortune of meeting the Campones.

When morning breaks, I'm green with nausea. I roll out of bed trying not to wake Sean. An eyelid opens, and a groggy voice asks, "Are you okay?"

Nodding, I tug on a robe and explain quickly. "Morning sickness. It'll pass. Go back to sleep."

Sean watches me for a moment. I feel awful, but his eyes say I'm a goddess. "I love you."

I smile at him, wishing I could say more but then feel my throat tighten and rush to the bathroom. After that settles down, I decide that getting sick with something in my stomach would be far better than dry heaving.

I head down the hallway to the kitchen. It's barely five in the morning, but there's a light cutting through the darkness. When I round the corner and enter the room, the sight surprises me.

Mom is wearing yoga pants and an oversized sweatshirt. Her dark hair is tugged into a high ponytail with wispy curls sticking out. There's a dusting of blush on her cheeks, and a sweep of mascara on her lashes. Sleep is long gone from her eyes. She's clinging to a cup of coffee, holding it in front of her and inhaling deeply. There's a soft smile on her lips. She's happy at that moment. There's no need to wonder if it's a fake attempt to be content just then. There's something about the sweep of her shoulders and the light touch of her fingers on the mug that tells the story on her face is real. She's far from all better—I've heard her wake in the night, screaming.

There's a long way to go, for both of us. Restlessness woke me and it didn't begin with morning sickness. Dreams churned into fear which twisted everything until I had a knife in my hand and watched Marty's eyes become lifeless. The dream repeats every time I close my eyes. Out of all my sins that one I regret the most. I was wrong about him. Marty played his hand so well that I couldn't tell which side he was on until it was too late.

Sitting opposite from Mom is Constance in her blood red dupioni silk robe. It has a floral pattern woven into the thick damask. Velvet lined lapels extend down to a thick scarlet sash tied tightly around her narrow waist. Constance's hair is a mess, one side flat with the other side still kempt as if she slept on that one side all night.

They stop talking and turn to watch me. Mom smiles. "How's my baby this morning?"

Constance smirks and adds, "You look awful. Saltines are on the counter."

Mom glances at me again and corrects Constance. "She doesn't look awful. Avery's glowing."

"Because she just vomited," Constance replies with a flick of her eyes. "Make sure you brush and floss every time you wretch or your teeth will rot. Then the dentist will tell me he thinks your bulimic and the newspapers will have a field day and blame me." She rolls her eyes and then sips her coffee.

Mom nods in agreement before she sees me still standing in the doorway and lifts her mug. "Do you want some coffee, honey?"

I shake my head and go straight for the box of crackers before sitting down next to both of them. I pull one out from the plastic wrapper and suck on it. Constance glares in disapproval. I glare at her and take the cracker from my mouth.

"Yes?" I dare her to say one more comment on dental hygiene or morning sickness.

"Nothing, dear." She smirks at Mom and takes another sip of coffee.

I ask my mother, "What do you have planned for today?" I shove another cracker into my mouth and slouch forward. Constance's perfect posture makes mine seem like an aerodynamic granny.

"We're planning to go shopping. Constance made us an appointment at one of those little boutiques. I want a poet's shirt with lace." She grins broadly and wiggles her fingers just below her chin, indicating a lacey neckline.

Constance snorts. "You're lucky that style made a comeback or we couldn't be seen together. If I have a hippie friend, people will talk. Suddenly everyone will think I've gone soft."

I laugh from behind my crackers, "No one will ever think that. Like ever."

Constance puffs up, proud. "Well, it doesn't matter what other people think."

"Oh really?"

She eyes me. Her long tapered fingers and ruby polish are immaculate. "I'm completely serious. I earned my reputation protecting my family. You've done the same. People will define you in ways that are unbecoming. Just look at what the chatter about you—"

Mom must have kicked her because Constance suddenly stops talking.

I flick my gaze to Mom and then Constance, and then back to Mom. "Why, what are people saying about me?"

Mom tries to soften it. "Your parentage is being discussed, and the disappearance of your only sibling is creating gossip."

"Ma, I don't care what they think, but I still want to know. Vic was an abomination, and I'm not sorry that he's gone. I guess that makes me a monster." A frown twists my lips as I stare at my row of crackers.

Constance snorts. "A monster? You?"

I lift my eyes, not shying away from my thoughts. I know what I did. I'm just not certain who I am because of it. Confessing bluntly, I admit, "Yeah, me. I lost it that night. I let the beast off the leash."

Constance starts laughing, and it's a high-pitched giggle. She presses her fingertips to her mouth after putting down her cup of coffee so that it won't spill. She places a hand on my arm. "Your beast is not a monster. It's a character trait many people wish they had. You're the girl who stood up to Satan and walked away."

"Right, but at the same time, doesn't the person who killed the devil become the devil?"

"No," Constance snaps, entirely confident. "It's not as if he were possessed by an evil spirit that now resides in you. Vic was a man, a deranged one, but his decisions were his own. His sins don't flow into your hands."

I realize that I don't believe her. I twist in my chair, not liking this topic of conversation, but I manage to spit out what's been keeping me awake. It's a tiny thought, one that will fester and putrefy if remains unaddressed. "Vic became who he was because of me. If I hadn't—"

Mom cuts me off, her hand suddenly on mine, possessive and assuring. "If you hadn't been born? You can't think like that. You did nothing to make him that way. Vic made his choices, and you made yours. You are not responsible for his actions. Sometimes people become so fixated on one thing. They think that their life would be better if this person didn't exist. It poisons the well and seeps out into every aspect of their life. Blaming someone for your shortcomings is easy. Looking in the mirror is not. Avery, you spend more time examining yourself and your motives than anyone. You've tried to stay true to yourself, and you have. What do you care about more than anything?"

I swallow hard and blink back the tears in my eyes. "My family. But Mom—"

She pats my hand and squeezes. "And you saved yours. If you didn't directly challenge Vic, I'd still be locked in that godforsaken basement. You saved me." There are tears in her eyes. It's the first time she's talked about any of this with me.

Constance leans back in her chair and adds, "You saved my clan as well. That makes your loyalty unquestionable. You're family, Avery. I hope you didn't have plans on leaving because now you're one of us. I meant it when I said that the other night. As far as I'm concerned, you earned the name Ferro."

Tears well up and I start sobbing. Before I plaster my hands over my eyes, Mom and Constance exchange a horrified expression.

Mom's hand is on my back. She's crouching next to my chair, trying to comfort me. "Honey, what is it? What's wrong?"

I'm completely crazy on the inside. I should be happy. Why the hell am I crying? "I don't know!"

I feel Mom smile as she holds me tight against her. She runs her hand over my hair and sings a song from when I was a little girl. When she finishes, she adds, "I know why you're crying. You thought you lost everything, but you haven't. Coming to terms with that fact is giving me issues too."

Constance blurts out, "Plus you're pregnant, and your hormones are rapidly changing. Everything is going to feel paramount, even little things. Don't explain yourself. You don't have to—not to us or anyone else for that matter."

Mom kisses the top of my head and squeezes me. "I love you."

"I love you too. I wish Daddy were here. I keep thinking that and it feels like I'm an ingrate." I pull back and swat at my tears. "I miss him."

Mom's eyes are glassy. She nods for a moment, unable to speak.

Constance leans forward and asks, "Tell me about him. I want to hear everything."

It's not until hours have passed and Sean is up that I realize what Constance gave us. Mom and I were able to talk about Daddy together, grieve his loss, and smile at his memories. Sharing a life doesn't stop when that person is gone. I'm my dad's girl. Victor Campone may be my biological father, but I will always be Ray Stanz's daughter. His strength, laughter, and grit flows through my veins. I never noticed how much I'm like him.

In this moment, who I am and who I will always be, emerges from the shadows. The demons that have been at my heels for so long, waiting for me to fall and devour my remains are dispelled. Now, in the early light of dawn, they slither away. There's a certainty to life that was missing for so long, a piece of knowledge that whispers today will come and go, the sun will rise and set, and I will still be breathing. The shadows that once clung to me so fiercely peel away. The crushing tightness in my chest recedes, the weight vanishing so that I can finally breathe again.

I know exactly who I am and what I'm capable of—Sean was right about that. People reveal their true nature at times of duress—some fall apart when pressed, while others turn rancid. My hands are stained with the blood of friends and foes—and I can live with it. I don't need to worry about devolving into a monster or becoming the likes of the Campones. I'm a Stanz and a Ferro through and through.

CHAPTER 22

The powdery sand clings to the soles of my feet as I pad down the long strip of beach. I adjust my sarong around my hips, tugging at the knot when the wind threatens to whisk it away. Sunglasses shield my eyes from the golden light as the sun reaches its apex in the cloudless azure sky. A sheet of turquoise water stretches past the horizon to my left. The occasional sandbar peaks out from the surface of the tranquil sea. Scattered palm trees surround the large home behind me. It's the only house on the entire island.

This isn't Manhattan. No, we left that world far behind. It's not that I never want to see that place again—I do—it's just that the one thing I wanted most was time alone with the people I love with no press badgering us. There's a shit-ton of drama waiting for me when we get home. I'm the sole heir to the Campone empire, marrying into the Ferro family, and I survived the wrath of Vic Jr. One of those things would make me the talk of every paper and television show—but all three? That threw me into a frenzied media limelight. Constance shielded me as much as possible, but whenever we left the building, there were reporters in tow.

As more information came to light, it intensified. An increasing number of disturbing incidents involving my biological brother surfaced. Let's just say I'm glad I went mental that night and fought like it was the end. If I hadn't, if Vic had captured me instead—I wouldn't have recovered. His hatred was aimed directly at me. He blamed me for everything. There wasn't a rational thought left in that man's mind.

As I sweep my toes through the sand, I wonder if I changed that much. On this island, with no one but Sean, I have time to think. I don't hide from my thoughts, which made them less turbulent as the days stretched into weeks.

Mom and Constance were here with us at first. Sean suggested escaping for a while, and Constance revealed she had a private island in the South Pacific. She described the house and the beach—said that there was an airstrip big enough to accommodate the jet. It was a chance to have some downtime and escape the tumultuous life that fell on our shoulders.

Mom was the first to agree to it. She lingered inside and at the infinity pool by the house. She did regular Mom things and cooked even though the home was fully staffed. The fridge was magically full of food and Mom prepared a feast that first day there. I think baking offered her some solace and gave her a place to vent her feelings. Just about every dish she made was thoroughly beaten with a meat tenderizer first whether it was needed or not.

Constance was either in the kitchen talking to Mom or on the pool deck. Although she always had a book or magazine in her hands, I rarely saw her reading. She watched the horizon most days, lost in thought. If Constance did that too long, Mom showed up and suggested a diversion. We all have to face our struggles alone, but we heal better together. The day before yesterday, they collected shells to take back to New York. Mom wanted to fill a jar with them. After a couple of weeks, they decided to return to life. Not that they were both fine now, but they'd had enough downtime and were ready to resume some semblance of normalcy. Sean and I lingered, staying behind.

As I approach the cabana, the gauzy curtains billow in the breeze. Sean is stretched out on a teak chaise with a newly acquired waterproof e-reader in one hand and the other tucked behind his head. His dark hair is damp, slicked back from his face. Those sapphire eyes are concealed by smoky sunglasses. A dusting of dark stubble lines his jaw. There's an empty lounge chair next to him, topped with a fluffy white towel and a book that fell into the ocean one too many times. The pages are wrinkled, and making it appear to be more of an albino bat than a piece of bound literature.

Sean glances up at me. "Good afternoon, Miss Smith." He puts his tablet on the table between the two chairs, rises and strides toward me. His chest gleams in the midday sun, each muscle well-defined and covered in a thin sheen of sweat. A pair of board shorts cut to mid-thigh cling to his hips in a bright blue that matches the ocean. A smirk curls his lips as he steps toward me and opens his arms.

"You look beautiful today, Mr. Jones." I step into the space, and close my eyes, basking in the sensation of being in his arms—in this once forbidden spot close to his heart.

For Sean, this embrace meant everything. He didn't let anyone in. Now he holds me here and welcomes me to stay. The walls that cracked and fell back in Manhattan didn't jut back up. Sometimes I can tell he's fighting the instinct that was once responsible for his wellbeing. If Sean didn't have thick defensive barriers, he wouldn't have survived.

A pleasant sound escapes from my mouth as I sigh against his chest and feel the warmth of his body. "I still can't believe we're here."

He keeps his strong arms wrapped around me, holding onto me like he'll never let go. "I know. All I've ever wanted was to have you all to myself, with no distractions, no family drama, and no limits."

I pull back and study him. Arching an eyebrow, I ask, "No limits? You never had any limits with me, remember? Miss Black talked me into checking everything on that sheet." I make a face and add, speaking more to myself than him, "Now that I Googled that stuff, I'm not sure what I was thinking there."

Sean laughs as he steps back and slides his hands down my arms. He tips his head to the side, indicating we should walk over to the shade of the cabana. We both sit on his chaise, hip to hip.

I bump my knee to his. "So, what are you reading? The Wall Street Journal? The Tediously Dreary Report by Bryan Boring?"

He grins sheepishly and reaches for his e-reader, which was not a typical expression for him. That peaks my interest. So does the speed that he moves, trying to get it before I do. I lunge for the device, curious. The mirth on his face coupled with a tinge of, what—

shame? He almost appears bashful. I grab the tablet first and turn it on.

Sean represses a grin before he simply states, "Don't judge me."

The book opens, and I scan the page before I click the top of the screen to read the title. My eyebrows rise into my hairline. My jaw drops and I gape, unable to speak. I know which book this is, but I have no idea why he's reading it.

Sean squirms uncomfortably before plucking the device from my hands. "Don't look at me like that."

I find my words and try hard not to laugh, but I can't contain my smile. "Since when do you read smut, Sean Ferro?"

"I thought I'd try something different."

I'm still gaping, shocked. "You can say that again. Why'd you pick that book? It's almost erotica."

A delighted grin lights up his face with a smile so seductive it's difficult to look anywhere else. "Because you were reading it. And it is a really dirty book. Too bad you didn't get to the ending." He waggles his eyebrows at me as he tries not to laugh.

I gape for a split second. When I slap it shut, I ask, "How'd you know that I didn't finish it?"

Sean smirks as he talks with his hands. "I saw it in your dorm room and it was in the same sorry state as that poor bastard." He points to the water-logged, half sun-dried novel on my chair. "The last few pages were stuck together, but the front of the book had apparently been thumbed through more than once. I wanted to see what captivated your attention so much."

I shrug and glance over my shoulder at him, answering seriously. "I don't know. It's romantic. The idea of no secrets and not taking anything off the table."

Sean leans in close, catches my eye. "I've been thinking about that."

"Have you?" I hold his gaze and wonder what's gotten into him. Since we got here, we've been together a few times, but he appears like he's been holding back.

"Yes." There's a sense of hesitation there, the tiniest bit of worry creasing his brow. "And I'd like to propose a plan of action for our more amorous activities."

"Really?" I don't say more because I have no clue where this conversation is going.

I've been worried he wouldn't touch me for nine months, but Sean hasn't made me believe we'd be celibate. We both have a lot of things to work out. It won't all just fall into place in a few days. When tons of bad things happen all at once, it screws with a person. Neither one of us was immune to that. We've both woken screaming, trapped in a dream that was all too real. But since we stepped foot on the sand, those nightmares lessened. I can sleep in his arms whether we're in the house or on the beach.

Sean presses his lips together and puts the device down before turning to face me. "I think we need a new arrangement."

"Oh?" I ask trying to hide the unnerved feeling from my face.

He nods and takes my hands in his, rubbing his thumbs along the back of my hand. He tips his head back slightly almost austere. "I do. Things have changed since we made the first agreement. Significantly."

Worry wrinkles my brow. I'm not sure I have much more to give in this department. Sean is already so dark in the bedroom, and while there's a lure to that, I'm not sure I can go darker. I can't fathom what's left that we haven't done.

Caution fills my voice even though I try to sound chipper to hide my worries. "What'd you have in mind?"

Sean swallows hard, and when he doesn't immediately blurt out the answer, I lean in and lift the sunglasses from his eyes and place them on the table to my side. Whatever it is that he has to say is weighing on him. Sean usually isn't so cautious with his words. It seems like now that he started the conversation, he wishes he hadn't.

When I face him again, I offer, "You can tell me anything. I want to know what you're thinking about, especially with this part of our relationship."

Pressing his lips tightly into a thin line, he nods once, tightly. Sean pushes his palms on his knees and rises. He turns away from me, runs a hand through his thick hair, and sucks in a jagged breath. When he turns and looks down at me sitting on the chaise, he confesses, "I know I've said things and led you to believe I wasn't interested, but it's something we skipped over—something I desperately want with you."

"What do you mean?"

"Avery, that night in the cabin, before things got dark, where we were just there—in the moment. I traced your curves and learned the feel of you. There was a softness to it that I wasn't interested in at the time, but I am now."

I try not to smile. My voice comes out small, "You are?"

He nods. "There's an immensely potent draw to discovering what makes you moan and brings you to the edge. I want to try the soft touches and the teasing seduction. The fear that was once required has fallen silent."

I stare up at him, shocked.

Sean continues, "It doesn't beckon me the way it once did. This new desire has sprung up in its place. I've been worried about telling you because I made such a big deal about not going this route in the past. I said traditional sexual acts were off limits, that I didn't want to go down this road again. The thing is, it's not plain—not with you. It's enticing and it calls to me in a way I can no longer ignore. There's something sublime in the act of mutual submission that I was blind to before, but I see it now. I was afraid you'd think I was a flake for even suggesting it. Maybe I'm not capable of tenderness like that at this point—I don't know—but I want this with you. I want to try."

When he glances up from under those dark lashes, clear blue eyes meet mine. Sex has always been a recreational activity for Sean, and when it started to feel like something more, one of us ran. We'd never willingly, knowingly entered the bedroom with this mindset. He's right, from day one it wasn't something he wanted or offered. It wasn't something I was interested in, but now that he's suggested it—I can't breathe.

My heart twists in my chest, half fearful and half elated. My lips part and when I try to speak, no words come out. I flap my jaw and move my arms, trying to tell Sean. It's like I took a brick to the head and am trying to figure the square root of three. Nothing comes out but incoherent sounds.

That's when Sean steps forward and takes my hands in his, and assures me. "Nothing has to change. We can keep things the way they are. I was just wondering if you liked having your neck kissed…wondered if you'd stay or push me away. Wondered if you'd—well, what you'd do if you weren't tied up." He smiles briefly, but it falls away in disappointment when he thinks I'm not interested in discovering those things with him. "It's okay, Avery."

Holy! Words! Talk! Move your mouth and make words! The chick living inside my head is beating my brain with a broom trying to prod me to speak.

I finally move and lean to the side to catch Sean's eye before he backpedals and convinces himself he shouldn't have said anything. "Hey, I've wondered that too."

"You did?"

I nod quickly. "Yeah, of course, I did. I just didn't think you were interested in all that stuff. I mean, it's not as exciting as having someone under your complete control, is it?" An awkward smile falls off my face because I think it'd be utterly intoxicating to be with him like that. It's not something he's offered, ever. In fact, Sean made it really clear that he would never offer that kind of intimacy, so I assume my ears broke and I'm misunderstanding him.

The corners of his lips curl up into a boyish smirk. "It's completely foreign to me.

I don't know what you'll do, and that's the draw to it. I'm not sure if you'll push back, guide me, or what. It's uncharted water for us." He watches my face carefully, trying read my thoughts, but there's so much apprehension in that beautiful face.

A broad smile lights up from within me. My voice warbles when I try to agree, "It is."

Is this actually happening? Sean is dropping the rest of his guard with me. It's completely down, and as he stands there before me, I know he truly loves me. That's what this is about—he wants to show me— but our past arrangements have limited how we do that. Even when we moved past the contract, this aspect was off the table.

"Sean, I want a chance to know you like that." I bite my lip to keep from squeeing or crying. I'm in emotional overload.

Sean sees it and pulls me up. When I stand in front of him, he steps closer and slips his hands across my cheeks, tipping my face up toward his. Tears stream down my face as he confesses, "I'll love you forever if you let me. I want to discover you, who you are now, what makes your toes curl, what makes you scream out my name in ecstasy. I want to know you in every possible way. I want all of you, Avery Stanz—shadows, light, and glitter. I'll never let you go. You are the very best thing that's ever happened to me. Please let me show you how I feel."

Trembling works its way through me, but I manage to say the word that will start the next part of my life. "Yes."

AUTHOR'S NOTE

Thank you to all the readers who helped make Sean Ferro into a worldwide phenomenon. You may not realize that THE ARRANGEMENT tightly intertwines with the other Ferro series.

While you are not required to read these other tales to enjoy THE ARRANGEMENT, these additional series shed more light on Sean Ferro and the evolution of his dark character. He appears in each series, playing a crucial part in each book, but never in the limelight.

The one series where Sean can be seen coming out of the shadows to protect his family is THE PROPOSITION. While this isn't a fluffy romance, it shines a light on Sean's emerging role within his family. I personally love to see the things going on in the background, the events that caused a character to grow. Sean was in a familial powder keg during his early relationship with Avery. It sets the tone for his actions and explains why he disappears from time to time in the books. If you wanted to know where Sean went and what he was doing, I've included a free sample so you can check it out.

Thank you so much for reading! I can't tell you how much I appreciate you. I look forward to writing more books for you in the coming years.

THE PROPOSITION

Chapter 1

The sky is clear except for a few white glittering stars. They're hung high out of reach, impossibly beautiful and distant. The air has that crisp fall scent, and I know there will be frost tonight. Dad would have covered his plants with plastic to get a few more weeks from their fragile lives. The tarp is in the basement, still folded, where he kept it. The pansies will freeze and fade. This is their last night in this house, as it is mine.

Pushing the swing on the back porch with the tip of my foot, I start it swaying again. Life is so fleeting, so meaningless. The hole that's swallowing me is relentless. I thought I'd cry more, but I haven't even been able to do that. The tears won't fall. Neil says it's because my father's death hasn't hit me yet, but it has. The weight of his loss presses so hard on my shoulders that I can't lift my face from the dirt. For all those years, it was just the two of us. He was always there for me. He saved me from incomprehensible misery and now that he's gone, I find myself back in the shadows, unable to escape.

My eyes sweep over the wooden fence, taking in the rotten boards. Things were tight and I knew Dad sacrificed for me, but I had no idea how much until now. My college bills, my car, and all the things I needed were paid for without a blink, but I never stopped to wonder where the money came from. Dad worked hard, so I assumed it was enough.

I was wrong.

There hadn't been enough for a long time, and I had no idea. He never said anything. When I came home from classes at the end of the day, he'd hand me a twenty and tell me to be a kid and go have fun. He said stuff like that all the time. It makes me wonder if he knew what was coming, but there's no way he foresaw this.

When I came home from class last week, I found him in the yard, face-down in a pile of leaves. My throat tightens and I push away the memory. It's not something that I ever want to see again, but the recollection lights up over and over again in my mind. My senses are overloaded. I can still feel Dad's cold skin and the weight of his lifeless body as I rolled him over. The texture of his tattered flannel jacket is still on my fingertips. The sound of my strangled voice crying out his name over and over again still rings in my ears. It's been a long time since I felt so afraid.

For the first time in a long time, I am alone.

My phone is on the wooden swing and chirps next to me. I don't feel like talking. Silence has encased me in a tomb of misery since that day. Neil stood next to me and held my hand until hours blurred into days. He didn't want to leave me here alone tonight, but I insisted. It's my last night in this house. I'll never step over the threshold again. I'll never catch the scent of my father's aftershave in his little bathroom. All the memories will be lost and it will be like he never existed.

There's no grave in which to lay his body, no stone to mark his plot. Those were things I couldn't afford. It kills me to leave him in the morgue, and let them have him, but I don't know what to do. There's not enough money to change anything, so when I found out the mortgage also needed to be brought up to date or they'd foreclose, I collapsed. It was too much. I understand Neil's concern and he's been a good friend, but there are some things a person has to face alone.

This last night in my house is one of them. It's my only chance to really know and hear that Dad's gone. He won't walk down the hall and I won't hear his footfalls on the stairs. It's just me now.

Neil's text beeps a second time and I finally flick the screen to life. *Are you all right?*

No, of course not, but that doesn't change my answer. *Yes, I'm fine.* That's what people say when they're in despair so deep that there are no words. They pretend to be all right and hope to God that one day, they will be. The fantasy that there is a day somewhere ahead of me where everything will be fine keeps me breathing.

Call me if you want me to come over. Love you, babe.

Neil is great, but I have to do this on my own. Saying goodbye isn't something he can do. Besides, I can't crumble into his arms and fall to pieces. For one, Neil is in graduate school working on his shrink degree. He won't let me fall to pieces. Losing control is bad for the soul, he would say. I don't know if I agree with him, but right now it feels safer to sit in my somber cocoon and stare at the ailing lawn. I want to soak in every last detail and say goodbye before I'm thrown out in the morning.

When the chill in the air bites through my pajamas, I pad across the crunchy grass and head inside. My laptop is on the kitchen table where I left it. The screen glows dimly and I stare at my story. For the past few nights I poured my heart into this computer. I don't really know what I wrote or why I wrote it. The things in this story aren't recent. They're from a former life where I was happy, loved, and safe. I relive those nights, the ones I spent in Bryan Ferro's arms, doing things that Neil would never condone. As I write, I find that love has two faces, passion and companionship. The long lost days are filled with silly stories of things I remembered doing with my Dad—learning to drive and running over a Canadian goose. They're the things that float to the top of my head, so I write them down without thought, without judgment.

It was my life, and now it's not.

The story floods and overflows from one page to the next, shifting between joy and agony, pain and pleasure. Sunlight and darkness mingle, fracturing the foundation of my life. They spill out of me like a living thing that needs to escape. I can't contain it. The words block the pain that pierces my heart and drowns out the sorrow that never ends. I find solace lost in a world of memories, in a world that's no longer real.

I scroll to the bottom of the document and start writing. This is the end. The daydream will shatter after tonight and the morning will bring the reality of my life. I'm homeless. Neil is the only person who's offered me help, so I took him up on it. His face lit up when he asked me to move in with him and I said yes. But tonight, I'm lost in the past, writing about things that happened long ago. Grief pours from me in waves until I type the final word, but it isn't enough. The gut-wrenching pain that is at the center of my chest doesn't ease. I still feel it there, twisting and pulling like a demon is trying to suck my soul from my body.

My eyes can barely focus anymore. I rub them with the back of my hand and pull up the website I was looking at the other day. Confession is good for the soul and since my spirit feels like it's dying, I want to try it. Anything that will ease my agony is worth the risk. Every last part of me is drowning in pain and this little act could give me a handhold on reality. Maybe it's living in the past, or maybe it's because I know these things were real and it anchors me. The words do something, they mean something. The letters aren't something static, stuck on a page. They live and breathe. I don't know how to explain it and I can't verbalize what compels me, but I want to do it.

Staring at the screen, I wonder if I do it— if I hit publish—what trouble will this bring? It's silly to even think anyone will see my story. Odds are that it will fall into the vast wasteland of ebooks that no one ever finds, so what am I afraid of? There's no one to pass judgment on me, and if one person reads it—isn't that what I want? The confession? Maybe I should be talking to a priest and not pouring my tormented soul onto the internet. My finger hovers above the ENTER key. Neil would condemn me for this. I know he would, but this isn't for him. It's for me, and sometimes the only way to move forward is to take a good look back and see where you've been. God knows I've been through enough turbulence that I can endure this, but it doesn't feel like it right now. When the Sheriff arrives in the morning, I don't know how I'll manage to walk away.

My throat tightens as I mash my lips together and the ache at the center of my chest throbs. Inhaling slowly, I close my eyes and picture my Dad's face. I think about what he'd say. When I look at the screen again, I know what I'm going to do. Tapping the button on the mouse, I click publish.

Chapter 2

Pieces of my past tangle together inside my mind. Emotions, memories, and thoughts pass behind my eyes during the day and wait until night to unravel. Feeling frayed doesn't even begin to describe how I feel. It's as if a black hole opened up and swallowed my entire life. Suddenly, everything is uprooted and destroyed. There's nothing I can do, there's no way to change it. And the cruelest part is that I was spared. There's no family to comfort me, no mother to hold me.

Until now, it was just me and Dad, and I was fine with that. Actually, I loved it. I'd come home after class and talk about my day. He'd have dinner on the table and we'd laugh. Some people don't get along with their father, but I got along with mine. Maybe because it was just the two of us for so long. His attention was always undivided, singularly focused on me.

There's only been one other person in my life who treated me like that, but I lost him. Bryan Ferro was every father's nightmare, and every girl's fantasy. He was a bad boy to the core with a soft spot for me. That's another piece of my past that I'll never get back. But that's the past, and this is now.

Neil is my boyfriend and he cares about me. We've been together for a long time, long enough for him to know my quirks and not care that I'm a little bit nuts. The way I see it, we're all a little bit crazy, and that's what makes life interesting. Neil agrees, but it makes his life interesting because he wants to fix their broken brains. Me, I'm not like that. I see the things that he wants to fix as patina, a wonderful glaze of cray cray over an otherwise boring sculpture.

We're at opposite ends of the spectrum, Neil and I, but that's okay because we both care about each other.

Neil opens a container of my things and looks inside. There are small piles of boxes, stacked up like a fort in the bedroom. Considering it's a lifetime of clothing and objects, there isn't very much. Since I tried to keep the house, I sold off anything of value. It killed me, but the reward was worth it. I'd get to keep a roof over my head and my father's house. The memories would still be there for me while I mourned my Dad's loss.

I'd have a chance to go through his things when I was ready, but that's not how things played out. There was too much debt, too many people that he owed too much money to, and nearly every dime went to my education, which is on hold until I figure out what to do.

"Unpacking would be a good start," Neil offers and holds up one of my shirts. His sandy hair is brushed to the side and he's wearing a polo shirt with a pair of khakis. He's always dressed like an old guy. Think casual Friday at some firm, and that's Neil's go-to outfit. I thought he slept in those perfectly pressed pants until I moved in. It turns out that Neil is a jammies man.

"You'll get over this, Hallie." Over is the wrong word. I'll get through this, but I'll never get over it. Neil doesn't understand how I feel or what's going through my head right now. Experiencing loss and reading about it are two different things.

I nod because my words will be too sharp and he's trying to be kind to me. I see it in his eyes. "I'll unpack, Neil. I just don't feel like it right now." My butt has been glued to this recliner for the past seven days. I don't watch television, play on my phone, tweet, or do anything except stare out the window. I need down time, away from everything and everyone. It makes my life more bearable.

Neil sighs and shakes his head. "I wish I could make you happy."

"You do." The lack of emotion in my voice is noticeable, even though I try to convey some. I just don't have it in me right now.

Neil shakes his head, and walks over to the recliner where I'm sitting. He crouches before me and tilts his head to catch my eye.

My gaze had been unfocused, staring at the wall, until he did that. "It's been a week and you've barely moved from this chair."

"I know." But I haven't cried or completely lost my mind. I want to tell him that, but I don't because he'll know that I'm a lot more banged up inside than he thinks.

"Hallie, I bought you something. I wasn't going to say anything until we got there, but I know how much it matters to you." Neil looks awkward as he says it, his dark eyes shifting away from mine.

What could he possibly buy me? I don't want anything that's remotely attainable and Neil's strapped, so it's not like he could go throw around his millions and fix everything. He has enough to keep his head above water and that's about it.

"Oh?" I try to be polite.

He nods and smiles up at me, taking both my hands in his. "Yes, it's kind of an odd gift, but I know how much it matters to you, so I bought a plot at the cemetery. I know you wanted a grave for your father. They transferred the body already and finished the headstone today. He should be there now, if you want to go and look."

"Is that why his ashes weren't ready?" I sniff once, hard.

He nods. "Yeah, baby. I thought you needed a place to mourn."

The corners of my lips pull up and falter. "I don't know how to react. I wanted…" my voice quivers and I snap my mouth shut. Neil nods like he knows. I lean forward and throw my arms around him.

He got me out of the chair.

Chapter 3

On the way to the cemetery, Neil turns on talk radio. He listens to weird stuff—well, stations that I think are weird (nonstop POTUS anyone?)—and right then it's women's programming. They're discussing some new book that they couldn't get enough of. It's evocative and filled with steamy sex, enough to curl the announcer's toes, or so she says.

Neil reaches forward and turns it off. "Great. More literary trash. Just what the world needs."

I nod absentmindedly and draw lines on the steamy window, which is probably driving Neil nuts, but he doesn't say anything. The sky looks like it's about to open up. Big gray clouds completely block the sun and there are no blue scraps of sky showing. It's getting dark, fast. Neil leans forward toward the windshield. "This trip might have to be a quick one, Hallie."

I nod slowly as the car turns into the cemetery. The grass is bright green and seems to go on forever. There are too many perfectly straight rows to count. Alphanumeric codes are nailed onto trees on little plastic squares, directing us through the mass of graves and around to the newer section in the back.

Neil stops next to a headstone with my last name spelled out in large letters: RAYMOND.

My stomach sinks. Seeing your last name on a tombstone does things to a person. Normal people don't think about their mortality or death, but seeing something like that makes you ponder it. Add in the freshly turned earth and I feel sick. Mentally, I scold myself. This is what I wanted for Dad. I wanted to lay him to rest here, but I couldn't afford it. Neil has given the most generous gift imaginable and I'm afraid to get out of the car. I take a deep breath, worried that Neil is going to rush me, but he says nothing. After turning off the engine, he pockets his keys and waits for me.

My phone chimes with Maggie's ringtone. Maggie Chichilad is my best friend, and has been trying to get a hold of me all day. For the past week, she's tried to take me out every night and every night I've declined. I can't bear to talk to her now, so I get out and slam the door behind me to seal in the sound.

One thing at a time Hallie. You can do this.

Although I walk next to Neil, I feel alone. It doesn't matter that we've been dating for years or that he knows me inside out. Everyone handles death alone. A shoulder to cry on is nice once I accept the inevitable, but I don't want to accept this. I can't believe Dad is gone. Every day passes like the one before, with me sitting on that chair, hoping that this whole thing was just some horrible mistake. *No, Hallie, that wasn't your dad on the lawn, he's fine.* We all laugh and go inside the house that he still owns. I still have a place to rest my head. My memories still echo in the halls of that house, loud and clear, because I have a home if only in my mind.

So I sit and stare at nothing, day after day, waiting to understand a divine joke that I cannot possibly perceive, because no matter what the truth is, it's too hard to accept. There's no way that Dad would have left me like this, not after everything I'd been through before he adopted me. Ghosts from that time of my life had fallen silent, but now they're stretching their claws and crawling out from between every mental crevice in my mind. The past and the present blur together in a wash of apathy and agony. Numbness consumes me until I don't feel anything at all.

So it surprises me that my nose registers the crisp air and that my skin feels the slick wet drops that fall from the frozen heavens and splatter on my cheeks. As I step toward the fresh grave, I wish that we could have given him a burial, that I could have saved him from being abandoned and forgotten. But I couldn't. And if it weren't for Neil, Dad wouldn't be here at all.

Reaching for Neil's hand, I tangle our fingers together and swallow the lump in my throat. "I'll pay you back for this." I know how much it cost, how much he spent. Before this happened, I thought funerals were a part of life, that everyone had one. It wasn't until I was the only surviving heir that I learned the reality of the situation.

Neil squeezes my hand. I feel his eyes on the side of my face. "Don't even think about that, Hallie. I wish I could have done more, but this wiped me out. We're going to be eating hot dogs for a while."

"I'd eat dirt if I had to."

"Well that's good, because there's probably a lot of dirt in the cheap wieners." He leans in and kisses me on the cheek. "I'll give you a minute. Come back to the car when you're ready." Neil walks away, leaving me staring at my father's new home.

The wind picks up and blows the little jagged crystals of precipitation harder. Each drop feels like a tiny razor as it hits my skin. I have no idea how long I stand there. It feels too long, but not hardly long enough. I stare at Dad's headstone and try to accept that this is where he'll be from now on. I've not given much thought to an afterlife, but even if there is one, it still means that I'm here by myself for a while. I shudder and hold my arms around my middle, hoping that Dad isn't really in the cold ground, all alone. I couldn't bear that, and yet, I have to.

His voice echoes in my ears like a distant song. He'd tell me not to stand here and weep. He'd tell me things that would make me smile and tell me that we could get through anything. And that's the problem— the eradication of 'we.' With him, nothing could stop me. I planned to take the world by storm and achieve awesome things. But on my own, I have no idea how weak I am or how fast I will fade into nothing.

At that moment, I have no future. There's no picture of the life ahead of me or what I will become. My future has been wiped clean and I have to begin again.

Chapter 4

I lay next to Neil, facing away from him. We haven't been together since before the funeral. Sex doesn't sound appealing right now, and I don't really care why I feel that way. My assumption has been that I'll feel like it when I'm ready.

Neil hasn't pressured me, but I know things can't stay like this. He scoots up behind me in the bed, pressing his body against mine, and whispers in my ear, "It's Friday."

Friday is our sex day. Neither of us has to be anywhere in the morning and so it was dubbed as the most logical day of the week to be together. It's not romantic, but I don't mind. Actually, I had liked that it was time for just the two of us, no matter what was going on. Since Neil likes to plan everything, it's a double bonus for him. Sometimes he plans things, little romantic gestures, and I can tell that he's been thinking about being with me for days. It's sweet, really. Maybe it's a little OCD, but since I tend to fly by the seat of my pants, it works. Neil brings order to my chaos.

His breath hits my ear in a warm wave. "I don't want to pressure you, but sometimes the best way to get on with life is to resume your regular activities. We could try it, Hallie." He strokes the hair away from my face so he can see me better.

I don't feel like being with him right now, but I don't really feel anything. Maybe it's not a bad idea. Relationships are give and take, and besides, I can't leave Neil alone forever. He was there for me and I need to be there for him.

Saying nothing, I roll over to face him. It's nonverbal permission for him to proceed. Neil strips me silently, but I feel more like a patient than his lover. He says sweet things as his hands rove over my body and he covers me in kisses, before settling between my legs. Rocking slowly, Neil does what he always does.

My body responds, I'm wet, but I don't feel anything. I know he's there and touching me. The sensation of his hands on my bare skin registers, but that's all it does. So, I stare blankly and look away, wishing that I could lose myself and become so overrun with lusty thoughts that my mind would pull out of this eternal nosedive.

Although Neil does the right things, and touches the right places, my body doesn't flare to life. It's not enough to pull my mind back from the dark places that consume my soul. Neil's body is slick as he develops a rhythm, slamming into me over and over again, finally tensing as he comes. I hold onto him tight and stare into the darkness, wondering if he can pull me back from the abyss.

I'm sinking, I can't feel anything, and I know that it's getting worse. Apathy is taking hold and I can't shake it off. Neil kisses my cheek and gets up from the bed. A second later the shower turns on. He'll expect me to join him, but I don't move.

I lay there feeling the same as before—nothing.

Chapter 5

Sleep doesn't come easily, but when it does I'm sucked into the past. Bryan's strong arms are around me, his voice whispers sweetly in my ear as he does things to me that make me forget myself. Those hot lips press a trail of kisses down the back of my neck. His voice isn't an echo, it's real. For a few hours I'm lost in the past, doing things that I haven't done since. Bryan's mouth is hot and moist, making my body rage with lust.

"Tell me what you want, Hallie. Say it." Bryan's breaths are hot and heavy in my ear. He has me pinned to my bed with his hands holding down my wrists. He presses his mouth to the spot on my back that makes my hips move on their own. Gasping, I moan his name, and tell him. I say words that I've never said since.

EASY: THE FERRO FAMILY

PRE-ORDER IT TODAY!

NEVER MISS A BOOK RELEASE!

Text HMWARD (one word) to 24587
to receive a text reminder on release day.

READY FOR MORE FERRO?
DAMAGED 3:
A DAMAGED WEDDING

MORE FERRO FAMILY BOOKS

JONATHAN FERRO
~STRIPPED~

******

TRYSTAN SCOTT
~BROKEN PROMISES~

******

NICK FERRO
~THE WEDDING CONTRACT~

*****

BRYAN FERRO
~THE PROPOSITION~

*****

SEAN FERRO
~THE ARRANGEMENT~

******

PETER FERRO GRANZ
~DAMAGED~

*****

MORE ROMANCE BY H.M. WARD

SCANDALOUS

SCANDALOUS 2

SECRETS

THE SECRET LIFE OF TRYSTAN SCOTT

DEMON KISSED

CHRISTMAS KISSES

OVER YOU

HOT GUY

And more.

To see a full book list, please visit:
www.hmward.com/books

CAN'T WAIT FOR H.M. WARD'S NEXT STEAMY BOOK?

★ ★ ★ ★ ★

Let her know by leaving stars and telling her
what you liked about
THE ARRANGEMENT 23
in a review!

ABOUT THE AUTHOR
H.M. WARD

New York Times bestselling author HM Ward continues to reign as the queen of independent publishing. She is swiftly approaching 13 MILLION copies sold, placing her among the literary titans. Articles pertaining to Ward's success have appeared in The New York Times, USA Today, and Forbes to name a few. This native New Yorker resides in Texas with her family, where she enjoys working on her next book.

You can interact with this bestselling author at:
Twitter: @HMWard
Facebook: AuthorHMWard
Webpage: www.hmward.com

1711

62410242R00184

Made in the USA
Lexington, KY
06 April 2017